THE CONVERSION

Amanda Lohrey is the author of nine novels. In 2012 she received the Patrick White Award, and her previous novel, *The Labyrinth*, won the Miles Franklin Literary Award. She lives in Tasmania.

THE
CONVERSION

AMANDA LOHREY

TEXT PUBLISHING MELBOURNE AUSTRALIA

The Text Publishing Company acknowledges the Traditional Owners of the country on which we work, the Wurundjeri people of the Kulin Nation, and pays respect to their Elders past and present.

textpublishing.com.au

The Text Publishing Company
Wurundjeri Country, Level 6, Royal Bank Chambers, 287 Collins Street, Melbourne Victoria 3000 Australia

Published by The Text Publishing Company, 2023

Cover design by W. H. Chong
Cover photograph by Steven Castan
Page design by Rachel Aitken
Typeset in Granjon 13.5/18.5 by J&M Typesetting

Quotations from August Strindberg's *A Dream Play* are taken from *Strindberg Plays: 2*, translated by Michael Meyer, Methuen, 2006.

Printed and bound in Australia by Griffin Press, a member of the Opus Group. The Opus Group is ISO/NZS 14001:2004 Environmental Management System certified.

ISBN: 9781922790484 (paperback)
ISBN: 9781922791610 (ebook)

A catalogue record for this book is available from the National Library of Australia.

FSC
www.fsc.org
MIX
Paper | Supporting
responsible forestry
FSC® C018684

The paper this book is printed on is certified against the Forest Stewardship Council® Standards. Griffin Press, a member of the Opus Group, holds chain of custody certification SCS-COC-001185. FSC® promotes environmentally responsible, socially beneficial and economically viable management of the world's forests.

'Nothing important comes with instructions.'
JAMES RICHARDSON, 'VECTORS 3.0'

PART 1

the windows

1

They were almost at the edge of the town when they saw the FOR SALE sign planted in front of a tall hedge. Nick pulled over to park on the verge and leaned across her to peer up at the old church, his chin close to her cheek, his left hand resting on her thigh. How warm that hand felt, how firm and secure, how strong the current of his energy.

'Well,' he said, 'it's even more picturesque than it looked online.'

They climbed out and pushed at the iron gates that swung open with a resistant creak, and there it stood at the top of a steep driveway: a small, handsome edifice of sandstone and granite with a tin roof and an empty belltower. The grass around it was dry and trim, and they thought they might as well try the door, but as they drew close they saw the snake, coiled and sleeping on the worn sandstone steps of the porch.

'We could throw a rock at it,' she said.

'No,' he said, 'leave it be.' The interior could wait.

They began their inspection on the southern side, where there were three separate stained-glass windows mounted with sturdy iron grilles. While Zoe tried to make out the figures in the glass, Nick stood back, gazing up at the stonework, his hand cupped over his eyes against the sun. She remembers thinking that he still had it, a man of sixty-three with a certain charisma. He was slim and fit, and his cropped grey curls gave him a Roman look, like one of those busts in a museum. After all these years she still took a secret pleasure in looking at him. His face had a perfect symmetry that had long cast a spell over her, the more potent for its being broken only by one crooked tooth in the front that slightly overlapped another tooth, as if to frame the perfection of the rest.

'Look,' he said, 'the walls have been heavily patched,' and he pointed to where the sandstone blocks and granite chunks had been roughly mortared over so that some individual stones were all but obscured by the dun-coloured paste. But the imposing corner stones were in good shape, as were the buttresses, and the guttering around the foundations was a warm orange brick that Nick thought might have been convict-made. Two squat tin chimneys rose above the roof for ventilation, and at the western end stood the empty belltower, a rusted weathervane on top, fixed and still.

Behind the church there were sheep grazing in a dry paddock and on the far side of the paddock they could see a dense eucalypt plantation, rows and rows of identical trees with spindly trunks that rose up out of stunted undergrowth. At the eastern end of the church, presumably the altar end, was a massive three-panelled stained-glass window, and they wondered at the expense of this in a small rural church. They thought it must at one time have been a well-heeled congregation, either that or a dedicated one, but again the iron grille obscured the figures.

She remembers hearing a loud screech and looking over to a stand of old macrocarpa pines where two black cockatoos were perched on a bough protruding from the nearest tree. She can still see their black bodies outlined against the blue of the sky, the strength of their hooked beaks, the way they balanced on one claw and held a pine-cone upright in the other, as if it were a fruit. Then she spotted the others, counting five in all, a flock, and one of their favourite birds: so elegant in flight, so comically imperious up close. Nick thought it a good omen.

They turned the corner and began their stroll along the northern wall, until they came to a single bush of Scotch thistle sprouting from a crack in the brick gutter. It drew their attention to a rectangle of worn sandstone carved with the inscription

ANNO DOMINI

MDCCCXC

So, it was late Victorian.

Back at the entrance the snake was gone. Nick tried the door, a solid gothic arch with iron hinges and a ring of plaited brass. It was locked, and they stepped back to gaze up at the belltower, lingering in the bright sun, and he put his arm around her waist and smiled.

'Not bad,' he said, 'not at all gloomy.' Then she thought of those iron grilles that covered the windows. Not only would they be living in a church, it might feel as if they were living in a gaol.

Nick looked over to the grazing paddocks beyond. 'A graveyard,' he said. 'You'd think there'd be one.'

Zoe pointed down the hill to the iron gates. 'It's across the road. You didn't see it?'

No, he hadn't, but was glad to find it set apart. It was probably on a separate title, and so much the better. There would be visitors coming to lay flowers or chase up their family tree for want of something better to do. And besides, they didn't want to have to manage a lot of crumbling head-stones and funereal obelisks tilting at an angle, and those awful little kitsch angels with downcast eyes. No respon-sibility for the dead; he was not up for it. In his work as a therapist, it was enough for him to deal with the living.

They drove on into the town, only five kilometres to the north. Crannock was a small settlement that lay in the valley between two larger towns and all three serviced the coalmines for which the valley was known, though in recent years much of the surrounding grazing land had been planted with vineyards.

It was a Sunday and the local realtor was closed, so they parked around the corner from the Jubilee Arms, a handsome colonial hotel with timber balconies painted green and cream. Inside, the hotel smelled of disinfectant and beer but the dining room had been refashioned in an austere minimalism of black granite and stainless steel. The publican's wife was obliging and offered them a late lunch, and they settled to a grilled backstrap of lamb, simple but perfectly cooked, with a glass of one of the local reds.

They had driven to the church on impulse, with no appointment to inspect, but already Nick was feeling optimistic. On the drive back to the city he was in good spirits and announced that he felt somehow unburdened, though of what he couldn't say. Zoe was less upbeat. Yes, the church had been charming, and yes, it had a lovely aspect, but a church was after all a church.

'Meaning?' he asked.

'Well, not a house,' she said, lamely, 'not a home.' And then: 'I suppose it's been deconsecrated.'

Nick thought it likely had, not that it need make any difference to a prospective buyer, not unless they were believers, and maybe not even then. But the thought unsettled her. Surely the church hierarchy didn't just abandon these places? Could you pretend a church had never been a sacred site? There must be some ritual involved, some way of letting go. If they bought it, would they risk having a sense of trespass? Some of the congregation might resent the sale, might feel they had lost a piece of themselves.

There couldn't be much of a congregation, Nick observed, or the church wouldn't be on the market. And the few diehards left might have an initial reaction but others would be grateful to them for rescuing what might otherwise become derelict. In any case, this stuff was all in the mind and need not trouble a prospective buyer. Neither he nor she had had a religious upbringing and they would come to it unencumbered by habit or super-stition. There were Indigenous peoples who held certain waterholes, rocks or trees to be sacred, but that didn't mean they held any special meaning for whitefellas.

'That's different,' she protested.

'*Is it?*' And he smiled at her indulgently. 'You think it might have some ghosts?' he teased.

No, she didn't, but she did think they might have to deal with locals who had a psychic investment in not just the building but the site itself. It would only be natural. 'You're the psychologist,' she said, 'you've always main-tained that there's a psychology of place, that we become attached to certain places and go on inhabiting them mentally long after we leave them behind physically.'

Of course, he said, but that psychology was not fixed, it evolved. At the right time and in the right place, one attach-ment could be replaced by another. The church, any church, would be what they made of it, and what was an abandoned church anyway? Just a big open space with infinite possibil-ities, and it felt right that it should come to them at a time in their lives when they were picking up the pieces from their losses in the financial crisis. 'See it as a gift, Zo.'

And so buoyant was he that she felt it would be churlish of her to argue. With luck, this would be another of his enthusiasms, soon to be replaced by something more suitable.

2

When the great crash came she had felt the shock of it in her bones. Day by day as she watched their capital fall she felt she was being flayed, with each cut of the scalpel accompanied by a soundtrack of hysterical pundits and the full throttle of that word *volatility*. A surge in the blood, a snapping of synapses, an arrhythmic heartbeat. Breathless, she was breathless, and bleeding money. It was such an odd sensation; up until then she had thought she had blood in her veins but all along she had been stuffed with wet currency. And then the numbness set in, so that she began to float in a limbo of shock.

But Nick? Well, he dealt with it. After a brief period of outrage followed by a few weeks of listless funk, he rebounded in a burst of almost manic restlessness. He would not be defeated by this; he would not. 'And let's face it, Zo,' he said, 'we've become stale, stale and complacent.' An established middle-class couple trundling along in their comfortable cocoon, tut-tutting at the television and taking expensive holidays. But now they had to think again, and it could be worse. They were in good health, fit enough to start over, and here was their chance.

Yes, they would have to sell the house, a handsome Federation villa they had worked on with such loving care, but they could move to the country and become part of one of those charming little towns that in recent years were being revitalised. He could find premises in the town—the rents would be modest—and set up a part-time practice with a handful of clients, enough to live on, and she would not have to go back to work.

Zoe could almost see the fantasy of it appear in a bubble above his head and could only gaze at him with a mix of wonder and resentment. But hadn't he always been like this, and often to a maddening degree?

For a week she contemplated returning to work. She had only recently taken early retirement when the small firm where she worked as a solicitor had been absorbed into a larger one and it had seemed the right time, for she was jaded. For the past year she had felt the desire for something new, something vague and unformed, but when radical change presented itself she was unprepared.

Not so Nick. For Nick it was always about the possibility of the new. The world was there to be remade, over and over, and anything less was stagnation. If friends began to talk earnestly about their family tree, as they seemed increasingly to do as they aged, he would look at Zoe and roll his eyes. He had little interest in history and above all he despised nostalgia: nostalgia was a form of weakness, emotional and spiritual laziness. The secret to life was to live in a dynamic present illuminated by the light of the possible. And might not this attitude, she reflected, now prove to be a strength? And in any case, what other options did they have?

And so together they went online to look at properties in regional towns, only to be dismayed by how expensive these had grown. An exodus from the city had begun a decade before with the last property boom and the listings were discouraging: featureless suburban bungalows with double garages, blank-faced and bare, or workers' cottages of manufactured charm, a glassy modern extension at the rear and potted camellias on a twee little front veranda. But then Nick found the church.

Light, airy and affordable, it sat on a low rise with a view across vineyards that sloped down to the floor of the valley. Behind it was the big grazing paddock while, to the west, hills covered in ironbark and mountain ash rose in an alluring haze. 'Look how cheap it is,' he said: 'any other property with a view like that would cost a motza. C'mon, Zo, let's not live in some soulless developer's box—we can do better than that.'

After all, they had renovated before, more than once. He was a practical man with a workshop full of tools and, yes, it would be difficult but they had the experience and they had the smarts. A church would be the ultimate challenge.

'Sunday,' he said. 'We'll drive out to the valley and take a look.'

3

It was not long after this that Neville Glass came to dinner.

Neville was Zoe's oldest friend, and a favourite of Nick's. Together he and Zoe had attended a big government school on the outskirts of Penrith and there they had formed an unlikely and asexual bond. Often in their final year they would catch the train home together and walk the kilometre to their respective homes on a new housing estate where the bush had been bulldozed and the bare yards sprouted nascent trees along the edges of tidy lawn. These walks were a secret pleasure for them both; away from the school grounds they did not have to affect any form of mindless cool but could debate the strangeness of the world.

Neville came from a strict Methodist family where, he lamented, even the placement of a cloth on the altar was regarded as a sin of decadence ('sensory deprivation') and he had responded by becoming a dialectician; at weekends he would sometimes travel to the reference library in the city to read theology, the better to argue with his father, and he liked to rehearse these Oedipal duels on his walks home with Zoe. She can still recall a conversation about the proofs of God, and Neville's methodical rebuttal of each of them. There were five proofs, none of which she could remember now, other than that there was something called a First Cause, an idea she had recoiled from; it had struck her as fixed and rigid, like a wooden packing box, all hard edges and enclosed.

Neville was a streak—tall, lanky and a cocksure know-all—but also open and at times innocently childlike. And when she had hooked up with Nick, he and Neville had taken to one another on sight, not least because they shared an interest in what Nick referred to as the psychology of space. A town planner, Neville had studied in Berkeley with the architect Christopher Alexander, whose contentious theories on the subject interested Nick, for in his own postgraduate research in psychology Nick had written a thesis on the mind's spatial awareness and how it affects neurosis. There was too much emphasis on our management of time, he wrote, and not enough on the way in which the body related to the space around it. The key to feeling at ease in the world was in finding the right dimensions and the right orientation, as if the art of living were a matter of putting together the pieces of a three-dimensional jigsaw, a design in which all the elements were aesthetically resolved to a degree that seemed to Zoe to be quasi-mystical, a little on the fuzzy side, though Nick scoffed at the suggestion. Not at all, he said; it was as practical a science as could be conceived of, which is why it was such a big deal when architects and town planners got it wrong. In his work as a therapist he paid special attention to how and where the client lived, and he would begin by asking them to draw their childhood home. Then he would ask them to draw the home that best signified who they felt they really were. He had thought of collecting these drawings together in a book, *The House as Self*, but decided that, even while preserving his clients' anonymity, it would be unethical.

Zoe had never fathomed this theory of Nick's. She could see a kind of logic nestled within it but there must, she thought, be more to it in his own case, for since their very first house together—and they had bought and sold several—he had been preoccupied with remodelling and renovating. Nothing was ever quite right. Over the years he had acquired a workshop of expensive tools and he liked nothing more than to hover over market stalls that sold antique ones. For Nick, these seemed to have the status of magical objects; they signified the mystery of making, the promise of transforming the intractable into the pliable—and, ultimately, the desirable—and he collected them almost as if they were totems: a vintage wood plane, a collection of Wiltshire metal files, a German gouge chisel, a Japanese carpenter's ink chalk of carved wood, a Swedish cast-iron nail puller, and a handsome wood and brass plumb bob that he kept on his desk.

Zoe suspected that this preoccupation had something to do with Nick's father having been a spec builder of shoddy houses who had once been prosecuted for cheating clients. But that was a taboo subject, and in any case Nick was of the opinion that the obvious explanation for anything was never the right one. It might be a trigger for behaviour but there was always more, always something deeper that lay at the bottom of the psyche like crystallised sediment.

Whatever it was in Nick, there was something there that had to be compensated for, straw that had to be spun into gold, and it seemed to her that he could never quite free himself of it because for years this discontent travelled with him, lodged like a needle in the brain. It meant that they moved often, renovating houses, tearing down walls, installing new windows and redesigning gardens until, in his teens, their acerbic older son, Dominic, had begun to refer to his father as the Great Renovator.

Nick had been keen to show Neville the little church online, and Nev had been enthusiastic. The church was an intimate size, not too big, and the proportions were good; it had pleasing nooks and was well aspected. And thank God it didn't have a steeple, Nev said, and gave his peculiar laugh, a kind of hoarse croak that ended in a gasp. Yes, they agreed, a steeple would be too grandiose, and expensive to maintain since it was common for pieces to fall off. The image of a flaking steeple seemed to amuse them both, as if it contained some hidden joke.

'But the windows,' Zoe protested. 'All that stained glass. What on earth would you do with it?'

'Simple,' said Neville. 'Take them out. You can be part of the cancel culture.'

'Cancelling what, exactly?'

'The old naysayers, the sermonisers. The ones who told you not to have sex before marriage.' And he wagged a finger in mock disapproval.

'But that would be expensive, not to mention the cost of new glass.'

Neville merely raised his eyebrows in a gesture of mock disdain, and it soon became apparent that he was not all that interested in practicalities—that was Nick's domain—but in the *idea* of a conversion, in how to turn one thing into something else: 'Happens all the time,' and he waved a long, bony hand. 'Look at how urban slums have become gentrified. Old warehouses used to smell of wheat dust, or blood and bone. Now they're full of modish little boutiques and smell of coffee.'

'Not quite the same, Nev.'

Not yet, he argued, but the trend was there. Old churches were a relic of another era. Think of how most of them were positioned on hills, and it wasn't so they could be nearer to heaven. That was the official line but really they were laying claim to territory. When the European colonists took possession, they did it in the name of Jesus. The cross was supposed to cancel out anything that came before it, a bit like the way the early Christians built their churches over the old pagan temples, or the Mughals built their mosques over sacred Hindu sites. Never mind the metaphysics, there was a politics to it. But now the congregations had dwindled and the most important part was the graveyards where people were attached to family burial grounds. The growth was all in the modern evangelical churches, fitted out like concert auditoriums with stage lights and amplifiers. As much charm as a school gym.

'Yes, Nev, all of that.' She liked to hear him hold forth but still she held her ground. It wasn't at all like renovating a house, she said. There was all that vertical space, for one thing, and how would you fill it? And might there not remain an essential, well, *churchiness*? What she feared most was being stuck with a jaded feeling of the past, a lingering effect of grandiosity combined with an air of melancholy abandonment. And might they not feel that they were always intruders, always bending something out of its natural shape?

Neville gave his gasping laugh. 'No, no, no, darling— that comes with the iconography,' and he waved his bony hand again. 'You get rid of all that. Strip out the fittings and what you're dealing with is a glorified barn.'

For much of this exchange Nick had listened in amused silence but now he intervened. 'It will be what we make of it,' he said, with quiet emphasis and in a tone of mild irritation. And he frowned at Zoe as if to say: how could she doubt him?

But doubt him she did, and for a year they hesitated. More than once he suggested they make an appointment to inspect the interior and on each occasion she made an excuse. And still the church did not sell. From time to time Nick would summon it online and find it remained on offer. Good. He would persuade her. He would draw up a renovation plan and show her how it could be done. In the evenings, while she watched television, he would sometimes sit beside her with a blank A4 pad on his knees and sketch out alternative plans for a conversion. They could build a mezzanine where the bedrooms could go. They could enclose the baptismal alcove so that it functioned as an office. The sanctuary could be partitioned into a snug where they watched television, divided from the living area proper by some kind of screen.

She could see that, as so often in the past, he was becoming fixated. And all the while she was holding up an invisible hand, as if she could freeze time and delay the day of reckoning. And then there were lucid moments, when she was at work in the garden where, in the midst of pulling weeds, she would pause, and lift her head to frame the question, as if it had only just occurred to her for the first time. What happens now? Where do we go from here?

She had persuaded Nick to wait a year before they put the house up for sale: time for her to adjust. But this seemed only to bring on fits of irritable impatience. He began to have a recurring dream in which he stood on the top rung of a ladder, rubbing away at a grimy church window, trying without success to make out the figures in the stained glass. 'I don't know why I have this dream,' he would say, 'it's you who has a problem with the windows.'

4

It was late spring, almost twelve months since their first visit to the church, when Zoe returned to the town of Crannock. Signs of the long winter drought were everywhere, and the paddocks had turned a dusty dun colour. The vineyards were parched; despite their lines of irrigation they had an air of containment, of the barely manageable. They would survive, but only just. She did not stop at the church but slowed as she approached the FOR SALE sign, long enough to note that it now looked worn and that someone had put a bullet hole in the O. The hedge had grown ragged and the spindly grass behind the iron gates was at knee height. *Snakes*, she thought. She was glad she had worn her boots.

She drove on into the centre of the town and it seemed oddly familiar, odd because she had been there only that one time with Nick. She parked a block away from the Jubilee Arms, outside a kebab shop, its doorway a curtain of plastic streamers, its bevelled carcass of lamb revolving in the window.

It was a Friday and just after noon.

In the dining area of the hotel she ordered lunch at

the bar and waited, sipping on a glass of the local wine. At the table next to her, two young women in stylish gym gear were picking at their salads and leaning over their bowls in earnest conversation. The one nearest her had a lean body and an unusually prominent calf muscle that signalled a kind of tensile strength. The other was bigger, with generous curves, a suggestion of pneumatic buoyancy.

'I don't ever not eat a cupcake if I want it and I'm thinner now than I've ever been.'

'That's weird. If I just look at a cupcake I put on a kilo.'

'You have to go with your gut instinct. Your instincts are your best guide.'

She gazed at them as if they were creatures from another planet and tried to recall what she had been like at that age, trailing two restless little boys behind her. She had never worn gym gear.

Her fish arrived and the smell of its charcoaled flesh broke into her reverie, but by then the vivid image of her youthful self had unsettled her, so much so that she was unable to eat and she rose to pay her bill. 'The fish looks good,' she said to the woman behind the bar, 'but I've lost my appetite.'

The midday sun was harsh, the street bleached in a glare of white light, and as she walked to the end of a long line of shops she was grateful for the shade of the old verandas, hung with pots of flowering shrubs.

Inside the real estate office she introduced herself to the agent, Grant Ashton. 'Zoe North,' she began. 'The church.'

'Ah, yes, did a drive-by, did you? Lovely old place, isn't it?'

'I gather it's been on the market a while.'

'About six months.'

She knew it had been longer. 'Does it have a name? I couldn't see any noticeboard in the grounds.'

'Yeah, St Martin's. Unusual, that. It's usually Mark, or John, isn't it? Or James. There was a sign but the owner took it down, as you would. We've had a few lookers but no takers. Not everyone's cup of tea.' He pulled a set of keys from his pocket: 'I'll just lock up and we'll get going.'

On the way to the church Grant had a thought. 'I think your husband rang me once,' he said. 'Wardlaw. Is that his name?'

'Yes.' How had he made the connection? Had Nick mentioned her by name, and her reluctance?

'Said he was interested in the church.'

'He was.' Her throat tightens and the trees beside the road begin to blur. 'He died four months ago.'

'Oh, I'm sorry.'

'He was interested in buying the church but I wasn't. Not then.'

'Oh.' He nodded and stared ahead at the road. She could see that he was flustered, for he veered over the white line, but then, regaining his focus: 'I think your husband would have liked the church. He sounded like a nice fella.'

And she knew then that he was lying. Something in his tone told her that he had met Nick, that Nick had driven out on his own to look at the interior of the church with Grant. Of course, he would not have been able to contain his curiosity, and that would explain the detail with which he had drawn up his possible plans for renovation, the plans with which he had hoped to persuade her.

Concerned now to make safe ground, Grant began to ease into his pitch. 'You know, some of these old country churches are a bit ordinary but this one's a little gem, and a bargain at the price.' It was a shame, really, he said, in a tone of mock regret. The owner had started out with all kinds of plans but had run out of money and was embroiled in a protracted and expensive divorce. 'But the floor is sound, and the roof, and he fixed the guttering, and had the foundations checked to see if they needed underpinning, so all good in that department. Oh, and he's had the place re-plumbed and rewired, but no solar panels. You've got the heritage angle to deal with, a caveat there. No alteration to the exterior, or the site. You can't build a garage but you can pretty much do what you like inside.'

Did Grant have a handout, a history of the place? 'Ah, no, nothing like that.' He hadn't been long in the town himself and the church was on the market before he took over the agency, so he couldn't say, but he wouldn't be surprised if a church as old as that had been endowed by one of the local squatters. It was a coalmining area now but there had been big grazing properties in the valley for aeons until many of them were subdivided and turned into vineyards. 'Try the cathedral in the city,' he said, 'they'll know.'

They parked outside the church door and stepped up into a small empty vestibule of sandstone walls, bare save for a wooden plaque with a burnt engraving: *O Lord deliver us from our present fallen life.*

The nave, however, was furnished, though in an odd way: part church and part improvised squat. The church had a distinctive smell and she thought she detected a whiff of incense; something had seeped into the wood-work, candle smoke perhaps. A fine layer of dust lay on its surfaces, lit by rays of afternoon light that slanted through the stained glass to make soft mosaic patterns of colour on the wooden floor. She looked up into a high ceiling of exposed beams and vaulted trusses with an apex of around ten metres and saw that it was in good repair, and she was relieved that the walls were also in good order, a cream-coloured plaster, the lower part of which was lined in dado board stained with dark varnish.

The owner had installed a rudimentary kitchen in the sacristy, and a crude shower bay and lavatory at the rear in an arched alcove near the stone baptismal font. There was a plywood screen around the lavatory but no curtain across the shower. More surprising was that he had left behind many of the original fittings: a pulpit carved with sheaves of wheat and some mahogany pews pushed back against the walls which on both sides were fixed with commemorative plaques, the first of which proclaimed the foundation of the Mothers' Union in 1927. A strip of frayed red carpet ran down the aisle of the nave to the chancel where, to her surprise, the altar remained, carved from stone and set on a platform. It was bare, save for a moth-eaten red-wool hassock perched precariously at one end.

Behind the altar was an impressive wooden screen, three metres high. 'They call that a reredos,' said Grant. 'You could sell that for a bit. I know of one conversion where the buyer cut one up and used it for a pantry door.' He gestured at the air. 'All this carved wood, it's a lost art.' Then he indicated the sanctuary—'After you'—and they climbed the shallow steps to the altar. There she could see that the side panels of the reredos were carved with chalices, each encircled by a wreath of vine leaves.

'You religious?' asked Grant. She shook her head. 'Me neither. I don't know if it would be easier to live in a place like this if you were, or harder.' And he told her he had once sold a church to a woman who collected pictures of Jesus with his heart on fire and hung them all over the walls. '*Creepy.*' He looked around, as if appraising the goods for the first time. 'This one's a bargain. The churches are keen to offload these places. They have to compensate the kids who were molested.'

'Yes, yes, of course.' A sick wave of dizziness came over her, so that when she looked down at the altar steps beneath her feet they blurred like an image going in and out of focus, and she felt a sudden lurch of vertigo. Could she, after all, go through with this? 'I think I've seen enough,' she said, and managed a weak smile.

Grant nodded. 'Can't be easy for you,' he said.

Once outside, he pointed down the hill. 'There's a graveyard across the road if you want to look—not that you'd have to worry about that. It's on a separate title and the congregation bought it.'

'Another time, I think.'

And as if he had sensed her unease, he said little after that. A canny salesman, she reflected, who knew when to shut up. They drove back to his office in silence.

That night she signed the contact. She would tell family and friends that it was the only place in a good location that she could afford, but in truth she needed to exorcise a ghost.

5

The first time had been a sodden Saturday afternoon, one of those torrential Sydney downpours when the sky hangs low and is rent by lightning, and then suddenly the storm has passed and the sky is lit with a grey pearlescent glow. Zoe opened the front door and there she was, the girl, in a damp red jacket with drops of rain glistening on her high cheekbones and on the motorcycle helmet tucked under one arm. Wisps of black hair stuck wetly to her forehead and her heavy black boots were caked with mud and leaves.

'Hello,' she said, 'is Nick there?'

Hearing her voice, Nick came to the door and frowned. He was clearly displeased but turned to Zoe and introduced the girl as Sophie, the daughter of an old schoolfriend. They invited her in, of course they did, and Nick took her jacket and hung it in the back porch where it dripped onto the slate tiles. The girl laid her helmet on the kitchen table, a black metal ball with a jagged silver stripe, and something about it irritated Zoe. 'I'll just put that in the hall for you,' she said.

When she returned, Nick was staring at the girl and

listening intently, for her voice barely rose above a whisper. She had just bought her motorbike and they talked about why she had sold her car, and how she had left her job in a bookshop and was looking around for something else. The conversation, mundane as it was, had an edge to it, a dark underlying resonance. No-one in the room was at ease, least of all the girl, and certainly not Nick.

Around five o'clock he stood and said he would see her out because he and Zoe were due at the house of friends and must soon leave. Zoe left him to usher the girl to the door, from where she heard a kind of urgent murmuring, and when Nick returned to the kitchen he sighed and sat heavily at the table. 'Not good,' he said, 'not good.'

What wasn't good?

'I'll tell you later, when we get back from Leo and Helen's.'

They had been invited to Leo and Helen Bury's to admire their renovations, the principal feature of which was the installation upstairs, at the centre of the house, of a movie room. With some ceremony Leo had ushered them into a large, windowless space carpeted in black. There were deep sofas covered in red wool and the walls too were a brick-red and hung with vintage movie posters. The screen itself was enormous. Zoe had found the effect overpowering, dismayed at the thought that she might have to sit in the room for two hours after dinner and politely endure a movie, but no, the technology had yet to be refined, something to do with the speakers, and she had been spared.

Driving home Nick had laughingly described the movie room as an enlarged womb; all that was missing was an umbilical cord to pipe up the contents of Leo's wine cellar. And suddenly she had an intimation that he was about to bring up the church, and perhaps even to make a disapproving remark about affluence. She was fond of Helen Bury and the movie room had not been her idea but Leo's. But it was also the case that since their losses Nick had shown signs of turning into a moralist, of becoming sententious, and she changed the subject: 'Who was that girl, Sophie, who had turned up in the afternoon?'

'The daughter of an old friend, Bruce Crane,' he said. Bruce had sent her to him for therapy because she had abandoned her studies and become withdrawn. Can you fix her, Bruce had asked, as if she were a broken-down piece of machinery on the hobby farm he had in the Kangaroo Valley. 'He's a prick.'

'I thought you said he was a friend.'

'Some friends are pricks.' But coming to their house was a violation of the protocols and he would tell her so at their next appointment. He really ought not to have let her into the house but she had taken him by surprise.

'How does she know where you live?'

He shook his head. 'Perhaps Bruce told her.'

'In that case, wouldn't it be wise to refer her to another therapist?'

'Maybe, but I think I can help her.'

In the house she turned on the hallway light and he

turned it off again. 'Don't,' he said, and put his arms around her, and began to stroke her body with the teasing finesse that had long ago made her his captive. That night they made love with an urgency, a contained violence that she can still recall. It might almost have been a premonition.

Some weeks later it occurred to her to ask: 'That girl, are you still seeing her?'

'Hardly a girl: she's twenty-eight. But no. I referred her to Pat Kiernan.'

Rarely did she ask him about his clients and the truth was that mostly she didn't want to know, didn't want the misery of strangers being brought into her home where it didn't belong. By mutual agreement they maintained an invisible firewall between Nick's work and the home. Their equilibrium depended on it.

And then one Saturday afternoon she came home from the supermarket and there she was, the girl, lying on the floor of their living room. It was such a startling image, like getting out of bed for a glass of water and coming upon a thief in the night. The girl lay on the carpet, in a corner, curled into a foetal ball, and while Zoe couldn't see her face she knew at once who it was. The primal scene, as she now thinks of it.

What is going on here? she mouthed at Nick, who was sitting on the couch and leaning forward intently, his fore-arms resting on his knees. Finger to lips, he made his plea for silence, and she carried her bags of groceries into the kitchen and dumped them noisily on the table. When she returned to the living room, Nick was crouching beside the girl. She was sitting up now, staring at the wall, and he had his arm around her shoulder.

Back in the kitchen Zoe began methodically to unpack her bags. Rice, butter, cheese, bacon…The girl was clearly in a state; she would have to be handled with care. Nick would deal with it. Despite her visceral repugnance at the sight of the foetus, which struck her as a pose, she must not blunder in.

She went to the sink to fill the kettle, and after a while Nick came into the kitchen with the girl beside him, clinging to his arm. He pulled out a chair from the table and, pressing lightly on the girl's shoulders, pushed her down onto the seat. 'Would you like something to drink?' he asked, and she nodded, and he gave Zoe a look, a look that said: *Say nothing, it will be all right soon.*

The girl sat trembling, and barely touched her water, and after just a few minutes he moved around the table and stood behind her. 'Time to go, Sophie,' he said, softly. But the girl didn't move. Then, to Zoe's surprise, Nick put his hands around the girl's shoulders, lifted her up out of her chair and ushered her out of the kitchen and down the long hallway to the front door. There was silence, and then the roar of the motorbike receding into the distance. Nick returned and sank into a chair. 'Christ!'

'Nick, this isn't healthy.'

'You're telling *me* that?' And he laid his hands palms down on the table and sighed. 'She's very fragile. She's on the edge. She's refusing to see Pat Kiernan and I can't just abandon her.'

'Is she suicidal?'

'Yes.'

'Have you told her father?'

'No.'

'Why not?'

'Because it could tip her over the edge. She hates him.'

'Did he molest her?'

'She says not.' He sighed again, deeper this time. 'I've booked her into a session in my rooms. We'll give it another go.'

'She can't keep coming here.'

'Don't worry, it won't happen again.'

6

The day after she signed the contract on St Martin's, her son Lachie rang from Adelaide. 'I'm coming to Sydney for a teachers' conference,' he said. 'Just the one night, unfortunately. When are you moving?'

'Early January. Can you come for dinner?'

'Sure. Can we make it an early one? I still have some work to do on my paper.'

From the first Lachie had approved the idea of the church, but then he had almost always agreed with his father, whom he resembled: the same tall, lanky frame, the same sandy hair and aquiline nose.

He turned up days later, direct from the airport, looking tired and thin. They ate an early dinner and he seemed to revive. They moved out onto the veranda for coffee, and he settled into one of the old cane chairs and put his feet up on a low stool in just the way that Nick used to do. For an instant the resemblance was uncanny.

Over dinner, he had teased her about the church, about her 'late conversion', but then, sensing perhaps that this might be insensitive, had said: 'You're doing this for Dad, aren't you?'

'Not exactly.'

'Why didn't the two of you snap it up when it first came on the market?'

'Somehow we didn't get around to it. We got distracted. And I had reservations, as you know.'

They got distracted all right, and there was a great deal in the past year that she hadn't told Lachie about his father, the father for whom he was still grieving.

'Dad would have loved it. It would have tested out his theories, all that stuff about the psychology of space.'

'Yes, he thought of the church as a blank slate, whereas it seemed to me to be the opposite.'

But Lachie had stopped listening and was gazing out the window. 'What happened to your bottlebrush?' The big red bottlebrush near the fence had recently been thrashed by a pair of black cockatoos and a carpet of red blooms lay on the ground in an almost perfect circle. Not that she minded; it mattered more to her that the birds fed from her trees, the trees that soon would not be hers, and she thought of that first day when she and Nick had looked at the church, the cockatoos in the pines and the ground beneath them littered with the shredded remnants of their feast.

'Mum?'

'Sorry. I was having a flashback. Cockatoos,' she said. 'Black ones. They love the bottlebrush.' She paused. 'Your father's favourite bird. And mine.'

Lachie turned to her and looked suddenly grave. 'You'll miss this house.'

'Will I?'

'You and the old man did so much work on it.' And before she could respond: 'You know, I've been thinking. Dad really should have been an architect. Then we wouldn't have had to move so often.'

'I don't know about that. Whatever he did, he was never satisfied. He never got it quite right.'

'Neither do architects.'

'No, but they're subject to practical constraints, like budgets. Your father had a problem with limits.'

'You had to admire him, though. He always went for it.'

'Yes,' and she smiled indulgently at her son. Never burden a child with the full story.

'I was thinking the other day about the Zen garden. Remember that?'

'How could I forget.'

'Other kids had fathers who played golf or talked footy. Mine built a Zen garden.'

The Zen garden had become a family joke, only it had not been funny at the time. When their boys were small, Nick had got it into his head to build a Zen garden out of rocks and sand: 'the management of space in its purest, simplest form.' He had a strong dislike of traditional English gardens, which he referred to as chicken-in-aspic gardens, and the cottage they had just bought, with a view to improvement, of course, was full of exotics: camellias, roses, rhododendrons, geraniums, lavender, all of which he pulled up or dug out, along with the lawn.

When she objected that Dominic and Lachie would have no backyard to play in, he replied that they could play in the park next door, and she made no further objection, in part because they had inherited the garden with the house and she had no attachment to it, and indeed had a vague intention to one day turn it into a native garden. And besides, she knew Nick was going through a difficult time at work and needed a project, a distraction.

He had bought a large dinner tray and filled it with sand, then arranged and rearranged a few small rocks, like islands in a dry sea, until he arrived at a composition that satisfied him, after which he bought three big rocks and two smaller ones from a landscape-garden centre. And when finally, after weeks, it was done and the backyard had been transformed, and the fine white gravel had been spread, he made a simple plywood rake, copied from the internet. And he would get up early every morning to rake the gravel before breakfast, sometimes in straight lines, sometimes in whorls, stylised patterns that were supposed to represent the waves of the ocean or the currents of the winds. It seemed to have a calming effect on him. 'The blessing of my day,' he would say.

'Nick's folly,' Neville had dubbed it, and insisted on pouring a bottle of champagne into the gravel to christen it. Not long after, on a dare, the boys had ridden their bikes through the garden, doing wheelies to make their own patterns in the sand and, as bad luck would have it, Nick had come home early and caught them. He lashed out to slap Dominic hard across the shoulders, and Dom fell from his bike and hit his head on one of the big ornamental rocks. For a minute he lay there, crumpled on his side, concussed, and she had rushed from the house just as he came to and began to vomit green bile onto the white gravel, his body shuddering with spasm after spasm, so that she felt the shock of it in her own guts and thought she would faint.

The following weekend Nick dismantled the garden. He had a mini-crane brought in to remove the rocks and shovelled the fine gravel into his trailer. Two weekends after that he brought in a load of topsoil and planted native grasses. 'Just as abstract in its way,' he said, contemplating it with a kind of resolute composure, 'but more user-friendly.'

There was always a solution.

It was this uncompromising optimism that drew people to Nick. In another man it might have appeared naive but in Nick it had a quality of fearlessness, of generosity. He seemed to emit an energetic field that offered you an unspoken invitation, a promise to recharge your own jaded current, and if that energy occasionally went off the rails, seemed somehow too much, too extravagant, too willed, still you forgave him, forgave him his delusion that he could make things right. And yet, as a therapist, he ought to have known, or at least learned from experience, that there are only ever accommodations, only the best effort that never quite hits the mark.

'Mum?'

'Sorry, I was thinking about the church.'

'So who was St Martin?'

'A Roman soldier. An early convert to Christianity, notable for cutting his cloak in half to give to a naked beggar on a winter's night. Your kind of saint.'

Of her two sons, Lachie was what might be described as the good one, though he had recently moved with Alice and the children to Adelaide, just when she needed him. Alice's family lived there and her mother had recently been diagnosed with breast cancer.

'Speaking of winter,' he began, 'what will you do for heating? It gets cold out there in the valley.'

'I'll see what other buyers have done. But for now there's a slow-combustion wood burner on a brick platform. It's pretty basic but it will do to begin with.'

'The hot air rises.'

'I know.'

'You could install fans to circulate the heat.'

'I'll get advice. There's plenty of time.' Yes, the rest of her life. 'When are you coming to visit? I miss the children.'

'Maybe we can come at Easter. I'll talk to Alice.'

She hesitated. 'Do you hear from Dom?'

'Not in a while. You know how he is.'

Yes, she knew. Dom, the brightest boy, the brilliant one, had dropped out of his studies, developed a heroin habit, moved on to methadone and was managing a bar in Melbourne. She rarely saw him, but every now and then he would ring, and they would talk for more than an hour as if it were only yesterday that he had left home. And not once did she reproach him, because if she did, he might not ring again. *He will come to me one day and until then I have nothing left but patience.*

As Lachie rose to leave she asked him: 'What are you planning to do about your father's tools?'

Just before he and the family had left for Adelaide, together they had packed up Nick's tools, ready for shipment. Even though he had not inherited his father's practicality, Lachie regarded them with a reverence that was touching. They had stood together in Nick's workshop, and as she watched the son handle the father's cherished collection it had brought on a rush of tears. He had never shared in his older brother's mockery of their father's obsession; to Lachie the tools were emblems of Nick's optimism, his unwillingness to settle for the make-do and the mediocre.

7

It took nine weeks to settle on the sale of her home, a period she would later think of as her interregnum. In that time her nights were an insomniac stretch of irritability and restlessness, of waking around three, alert and with her heart pounding. Then she would resort to what she found oddly soothing; she went online and trawled through a Pinterest page on church conversions: *Old churches that have been turned into Heavenly Homes*.

There were hundreds of these, follies of all kinds: grandiose staircases, sunken gardens, trapezoidal windows and plastic domes. Solid cedar pews became kitchen benches and one conversion even had an internal swimming pool. There was the church furnished with red-velvet chaise longues, high-backed velvet chairs and heavy drapes with gold tassels; red velvet everywhere, and potted palms like the theatre set of a Victorian melodrama, or an etching she had once seen of the interior of an Edwardian brothel.

The sheer verticality of the space was a constraint, and a typical conversion relied on a mezzanine or cut the space into layers, which meant the floors were set halfway up the tall windows so that they looked somehow amputated.

There were modern kitchens, streamlined and shiny like pathology labs, in which vaulting spaces soared above the tiny induction hotplates and marble benchtops. No matter the style adopted, a lingering effect of disproportion seemed impossible to overcome, so that, despite limitless ingenuity and massive expense, the human occupants resembled small mammals scurrying across the floor of a gutted castle.

The most successful conversions appeared to be the ones without stained-glass windows: Lutheran, Presbyterian or Methodist chapels. It was easy to remove a crucifix, but the rich figuration of the windows was something else. It had already occurred to her that since altar screens brought good money at auctions, perhaps she could sell her reredos to pay for repairs. The website of Antique Church Furnishings in London had a screen for sale that was similar to hers, with a sheaf of wheat and a bunch of grapes carved into its side panels. It was advertised with the tag: 'would make a fantastic backdrop for a Christian bakery come off-licence'. This made her laugh out loud, though not as much as when she discovered a conversion online where a woman had converted a hulking Catholic confessional into a walk-in wardrobe. Surely the revenge of Eve?

And then there were the community-based conversions, like the medieval church of St-Mary-at-Lambeth in South London, which had declined into dereliction and been slated for demolition until a group of enthusiasts had turned it into a garden museum. The church was now an ark of plants from around the world with exhibition spaces and a modern cloister. Nature had replaced its Creator as the focus of visitor worship and yet, to Zoe's eyes, the place looked worthy but dull. You destroy the mystique and what's left?

8

She took possession of St Martin's in the New Year.

On her first inspection the interior had been clean, if a little dusty, but when she unlocked the big door and the removalists began to unload, she saw that one of the stained-glass windows had been left open at the top where the iron grille didn't reach, and a small pane of plain glass had been wound open on a hinge to let in the air. A pigeon had flown in and was lying dead on the deeply recessed stone of the window ledge. The bird had evidently been trapped inside for some time, for there was bird shit scattered on the floor and on the pews near the window. As if that weren't enough, a possum had managed to find its way in, perhaps through a gap in the foundations, and there were scats on the fraying red carpet that ran down the nave.

Lachie had flown in for the weekend to help her. He had offered at the last minute and she had said yes, with relief. The good son. The removalists, two young Sikhs, had unloaded briskly and she had carried the coffee machine in from the back of her car to set it up and make them coffee. They perched on the edge of the couch and the older one looked around him.

'You will live in a temple,' he said, solemnly.

'Well, it used to be a temple,' she said, 'but not anymore.' And was struck by his word: *temple*. How different it sounded from the more sturdy *church*. Lighter, it seemed to float a little above the solid ground.

After the young men had gone, Lachie carried in her suitcases from the car and they set about cleaning up the mess, then sank onto the couch and ate sandwiches and fruit because the dining table was covered in boxes and they couldn't be bothered driving into the town for dinner. Lachie lay back with his feet on the coffee table, nursing the glass she had filled with wine, and gazed up at the ceiling. 'I like it,' he pronounced. 'It has a good feel. I was worried you might have bought a dud but no, it'll work.'

Just after nine she made up the couch for him and he was asleep by ten. He always was a good sleeper, unlike his restless brother and, although she was bone weary, she forced herself to stay awake for a while, the better to gaze on that dear face.

On that first night she had died into a dreamless sleep, exhausted by the effort of arrival and happy to have her son beside her. In the morning they began to unpack some of the boxes, for there were boxes everywhere. What on earth was in them, she wondered. She had given away so much. They unpacked the kitchen boxes first and set up the sacristy, then drove to the town to shop at the local supermarket, after which they ate a late lunch at the hotel.

Lachie dropped her off on his way to the airport, promising to return at Easter with Alice and the children.

When it grew dark, she lay on the bed and stared up at the shadowy wrought-iron chandelier with its mock candles, a cluster of narrow pointed light bulbs that hung from a great height above her. She thought of the many brides who, in her mind's eye, were gliding down the nave now like a procession of white ghosts, their trains trailing along the red carpet, their fine net veils obscuring their bright eyes and rouged cheeks. Upstairs in a corner of the choirstall the bridal march droned out from an old harmonium.

'So,' she said aloud, 'here we are. You wanted a church, Nick, and here it is. And now you've left me in the company of St Martin,' and she looked over to the figure on the south wall, a mosaic of coloured-glass pieces held together by decaying solder: a sturdy figure in a tunic and plumed helmet, wielding his sword in the act of severing his red cloak in half for the shivering wretch naked at his feet.

In the morning she woke early with tears running down her cheeks and into the hollow of her neck. Outside, the warble of magpies rose from the dry grass, the piping effrontery of birdsong. Day one, she told herself, day one. She must get up. She must begin to unpack; she must not sink into a trough of dejection. But her body was limp, her limbs heavy against the humid sheet.

Then came the sound of persistent screeching, close

overhead, and she knew that sound, knew it to be the black cockatoos, and she hoped they were returning to the old pine trees. In her mind's eye she could see the slow, heavy beat of their wings above the roof, could see their claws fasten onto the protruding bough, and she looked into their bold, staring eyes. Then, with more of a groan than a sigh, she sat up and wiped her face with a corner of the sheet.

In the sacristy kitchen she made coffee and fried bacon, which she ate on the couch, her feet on the velvet hassock that she planned to wash and mend with embroidery cotton. The smell of bacon pervaded the church: she must soon have an extractor fan installed. She must make a list, but for now she was light-headed and almost disoriented. In need of company, she turned on the television. But how alien it looked, its pixelated shimmer dwarfed by the apostles in the window above it, ageless men in scarlet and gold robes with trim beards and the eyes of small boys. I will need, she thought, to find a cupboard for the TV, or a screen.

'A church will always be a church,' her sister had said when she rang to tell Isobel about St Martin's. 'The space you live in will change you, not the other way around.' And then the inevitable lecture from the older sibling. 'You crazy girl, you should have designed one of those mini-homes and started from scratch. Or bought a decent kit home and modified it, one room at a time. And what about all that stained glass? You can't modernise that.'

And it was true, and for now she felt like an alien who had crossed the border into a foreign country: Roman soldiers and Latin banners inscribed in thick Gothic script that neither she nor Lachie could translate. The evening before they had peered at each in turn and she had begun to read aloud from one of them: 'In memory of Reginald Lonsdale, 94th Regiment, God-fearing man and an explorer of West Africa in search of'—but she was unable to decipher the rest. And Lachie had laughed. 'In search of plunder,' he said, 'some of which may well have paid for that window.'

Right now the church was in need of a good scrub and she resolved to make a start. In the kitchen she filled a bucket with warm water and detergent and carried it to the nave. But this only recalled her to the week when she packed up her home in the city and the estrangement she had felt in dismantling her past, as if for the first time she saw through appearances to the unspeakable banality of the everyday: the half-full jar of chutney, plastic containers of frozen fruit, empty glass jars on the bottom shelf of the pantry cupboard, unopened packets of biscuits, the fifteen empty vases along the top shelf of the laundry.

When she had finished sorting and junking, and the boxes from the pantry were stacked by the back door, she took twelve of the vases outside and smashed them against the terracotta paving. Some splintered, some shattered, while the ceramic ones merely cracked into large pieces, like sherds unearthed on an archaeological dig. But each vase made its own breaking sound, its own cry of being unmade and undone, and each sound was in its own way satisfying.

By the end of that first day she had scoured the stone window ledges, mopped the floor, dusted the pews that were ranged against the walls and unpacked several boxes. With daylight saving it didn't get dark until after eight and she did not turn on the lights but instead lit some handsome beeswax candles that Lachie had brought her as a housewarming present ('Incense to follow'). The soft flickering light lulled her into a state of surrender that, along with the fatigue of her exertions, sent her to bed early. It will be all right, she thought, it will be all right.

But it was not all right, because some time in the early morning she dreamed of the girl. In her dream the girl turned up at the church door, banging pitifully and crying out for Nick. *Nick's not here*, she said, and bolted the door, but the girl began to beat against the windows so that the stained glass rattled and shook, and she saw with a start that the girl's face had appeared in one of the windows, only it was featureless, a blank of milky opaque glass.

She woke in the dark, in confusion, and reached for the switch on the bedside lamp. And sat up, in the flare of lamplight, as if to expel the dream from her sight. Not that the image of the girl was clear; it was more of a presence. She found then that she struggled to recall the girl's face, her face in real life, or rather she remembered bits of it but not the whole. Her hair was short, almost black, like her eyes, which were both vulnerable and angry, eyes that spoke of some grievance against the world, and of a fear that the grievance would never be acknowledged, that no-one ever would, ever could, know her. Or that someone had known her, but in the worst possible way.

Once again she had turned up at the house, and again on a Saturday afternoon. Only this time Nick was not at home. 'Nick's not here,' Zoe had said, 'and I think it would be best, Sophie, if you didn't come here again.' And the girl had stared at her, with an expression both delicate and forlorn, so that despite herself Zoe had been touched by her air of bewildered abjection.

The poor girl, she thought: what could drive her to this? And in that instant of hesitation, Lachie pulled into the drive with the children in the back of the car. Isaac and Tess clambered out and ran towards her, and threw themselves around her legs, and so pleased was she to see them that she forgot about the girl until she became aware that she had followed Lachie into the house. Faced with the possibility of unpleasantness, Zoe had relented.

They sat out on the back lawn with drinks and the girl was childlike, playing tag with Isaac and Tess in an unselfconscious and disarming way, guilelessly, as if in reverting to childhood she was herself again, a self somewhere between the overgrown foetus curled up in a corner of the living room and the young woman with black eyes and a dark, affronted stare. And Zoe saw that in a way she was still a child, saw a sweetness and a fragile intelligence, unsure of what to do with itself. And she knew then that the girl was not at home in the world but yearned to be, only the world wouldn't open to her.

'Who's that?' Lachie asked when they were alone together in the kitchen and the children were shrieking in zigzagging paths of tag.

'The daughter of an old friend of your father's,' she said.

Then Lachie, who had a nose for a situation, said: 'Why is she here?'

And Zoe covered for Nick, as she always did, and said: 'I don't know.'

Not long after that, when Lachie and the children had gone and she and the girl were alone together in the kitchen, she said, gently: 'Time to go, Sophie.' And the girl gave her sad smile and went without protest, which Zoe took as a good sign. If she were a hysteric, she thought, if she were fixated on Nick, she would have contrived to hang around in the hope that he might soon come home. But like an obedient child she gathered up her helmet and walked towards the door. Zoe held her breath, waiting for the sound of Nick's car in the drive but, thank God, nothing.

When at last he came home, she told him.

'Why didn't you tell her to leave?' he demanded.

'She's *your* patient. You're the one who's not in control of this.'

50

He closed his eyes and sighed. He looked tired, and she regretted her tone. For some time they had not been at ease with each other. An edge had crept into their exchanges, and they made love less often. She knew he was frustrated because she would not agree to make an offer on the church, and more than once he had reproached her for not coming up with an alternative. He at least had a plan, a vision for pulling their irons out of the fire. All she could do was stall.

9

February was hot. She had expected the stone walls of the church would be cooling but the opposite proved to be the case: the stonework absorbed the heat and there was no insulation. To achieve this she could line the current walls with insulating foam and cover that with plasterboard, in effect a set of false walls, but that would be expensive. It seemed that converting a church was all about getting the surfaces right and then deciding what to do with an excess of vertical space. Any other consideration fell into the category of personal style. All of this she would have to think through, but for now she plugged in two free-standing fans. She would get a quote on ceiling fans when she felt up to it. Meanwhile, she worked in the air-conditioned cool of the Crannock hospital.

The Crannock Medical Centre was a small subacute regional hospital with eight beds, two government doctors who operated a general practice and twenty-odd nurses on a roster. She had applied for the position of day receptionist soon after arriving and in her interview the chairman of the hospital board, Gail McVilly, a formidable woman in a floral kaftan, told her that given her former employment as a solicitor she was over-qualified. But they gave her the job anyway. Perhaps because she had started her working life as a trainee nurse they thought her unlikely to be fazed by any gory emergency that might arise, and they seemed to approve of her purchase of the church.

The hospital stood on the other side of town from St Martin's, set on a low rise near a patch of bush that overlooked the valley. On her first day there she took a byroad to work in the early morning, past houses set deep in the bush as if they had something to hide or were fearful of intrusion. Almost every one of them had solar panels, no matter how ragged their gardens or fierce their dogs. There was enough sun, day in and day out, to charge their black silicon panels while each month the grass beneath them faded to straw. And in the midst of them stood an abandoned cheese factory, a grey concrete box with broken windows and a crude Art Deco entrance resembling nothing so much as the opening to a small Mayan temple.

No sooner had she arrived, just after seven-thirty, than a well-dressed middle-aged woman presented with pains in her chest. Zoe rang for the duty nurse and when no-one appeared she walked the woman to the emergency room and sat with her while they waited. The woman was pale and anxious but, acting on experience, Zoe thought she would most likely be okay. Her old matron, Dottie Wallace, had several iron-clad maxims, one of which was that if they turned up early in the morning with their foundation and lipstick on, it was unlikely to be anything serious. At the age of nineteen Zoe had been surprised at this; she had thought Matron inclined to underestimate a woman's pride.

After a few minutes Dr Khalid arrived, a tall, slender man, in his forties, she guessed. Egyptian perhaps, or Syrian. She got up to leave and he said: 'Mrs North?' She said yes (she had never taken Nick's name of Wardlaw) and he said he hoped she would like it there. And she said she was sure she would. And he nodded and said, 'Good,' in a peremptory though not unfriendly manner and turned his attention to the new patient.

It was a quiet morning. The window of her office looked out over the valley, the strict parallel lines of grapevines, the narrow winding river, its water low from the long drought, its banks lined with clumps of river wattle and willow. To the west the undulating hills were framed by the shadow of deep ravines, and bald rock faces where abseilers dangled from rope.

She ate her lunch on a bench beneath the shade of an old chestnut tree where the sun filtered through the branches onto her bare arms. From here she could see the entrance—NEEDLE EXCHANGE UNAVAILABLE ON THIS SITE—should anyone arrive who had not booked in. Hung with pale green burrs of fruit, the chestnut was one in an avenue planted in 1919 to commemorate the great flu epidemic. The patch of lawn beneath her feet was strewn with small black balls of wallaby scat and she could hear the virtuous buzz of bees hovering in and around the flame-coloured blooms of the leucospermum bush nearby. The pincushion tree, her mother had called it, and she reflected on how handsome one would look in the churchyard, and yet so far she had not been able to give any thought to a garden there, which was odd since she had been a gardener all her life. For now, the domestication of that space seemed inconceivable. It was too dry for exotics and a bush garden would not look sympathetic; the stonework was too imposing. The big macrocarpa pines that had been there since the colonial era looked right; both the church and the pines shared a common quality for which there was no name.

It was ironic, she reflected, that she should work now in a hospital when as a young nurse she had lost her nerve, lost it when confronted by the violence of love. It had begun as an ordinary day somewhere in the middle of her second year of training.

It was a Wednesday evening just after six, and she was attending her first birth, a woman in her late thirties, a *primigravida*. After many hours of labour things had begun to go pear-shaped. The baby's heartbeat was getting fainter and the obstetrician, a woman whose name she could still recall, Fiona, muttered: 'This baby has to come out now.' Too late for a caesarean and they had to suction it, and out it came, purple and with the cord around its neck.

Zoe had her back against the wall near the door, and from there she watched as they put up a screen around the mother so that she couldn't see the resuscitation machine being wheeled in, but the father saw it and blanched. They laid the baby, a boy, on the bench and began to thump his chest. Still no heartbeat. Then, to her horror, Fiona lifted the baby in the air and gave it a gentle shake. Then back to the bench: thump the chest, thump the chest. Lift the baby: shake the baby. Back on the bench: thump the chest. The manic flurry of it made Zoe nauseated and she felt a lurching sensation in her gut. The violence of the scene, nothing had prepared her for it. From down the corridor came the rattle of a trolley and the insistent beep of a machine but here, propped up on a pillow, the dazed mother, the bloodied sheet, the turbid clot of the placenta in a steel bowl.

And then the team stood back, and Fiona said to the father: 'Put your hand on your son's chest and say something.'

The father, pale, in shock, did as he was told. 'C'mon, mate,' he said, 'I'm looking forward to us having some fun.'

Later, at the debriefing, Zoe had learned that with these words the little finger on the baby's left hand twitched ('voice recognition') but all she saw was the team lurch forward, roused to begin again, the mother dazed behind the screen, the father trembling.

The baby survived, unharmed. What had seemed to last an hour had not even been a matter of minutes. The midwife wrapped the boy and put him in his mother's arms. She smiled. 'We'll call him Royce,' she said.

That night Zoe had fallen into her bed in a fit of uncontrolled crying. *These people are strong*, she thought. I am not in their league. She must find something else to do with her life.

Through a family contact she got a job as a legal secretary and, finding to her surprise that she had a feel for the work, she enrolled in a study of the law at night. In the second year of her course she met Nick, who encouraged her to study full-time, even though he would have to support them both and it would delay the day when they could afford to buy a home. And so, to the surprise of her mother and her sister, who had always underestimated her, she became a solicitor, working in a suburban practice. She was methodical, she had an eye for detail and she was decisive. Before long she had become the repository of other people's secrets.

But that was some other woman. She checked her phone, stood and brushed the crumbs from her skirt. Her first day at work in three years and already she felt surprisingly at home.

10

By the end of the month she was more or less settled,
camping ecclesiastically, as Lachie put it. She slept on a
queen-size bed and had her leather couch, dark green,
with one deep leather armchair, an antique sideboard, a
coffee table, lamps, a dining table and six chairs, a book-
case, and a big Persian rug. She had brought with her a
favourite gilt mirror but had yet to hang it; a mirror, she
had discovered, looked out of place in a church. A mirror
was meant to reflect light into a space but the windows
already allowed the light in, and wherever she held the
mirror against the wall it presented a jarring adjunct to
the stained glass, as if her own image did not belong in this
place, as if the pious men who surrounded her would not
allow of her intrusion. Perhaps in time she would hang it
in the vestibule, where there was no window, but for the
time being she stood it on the floor with its face against
the wall.

The rest of her possessions she had sold. But the
thing was this: above her head there was too much space,
a volume of air that reduced her tokens of domesticity
to doll's house miniatures, except for the Edwardian oak

sideboard, so big and solid, so ornate and monumental that it looked at home in the church, like a secular version of an altar. She centred the sideboard against the western wall and stored her linen in its cupboards and her medicines and toiletries in its drawers. On one of its ornately carved ledges she put her perfume and face cream, and on the other a snake bandage. She cleaned her teeth in the sacristy kitchen.

She was not yet ready to put up a photograph of Nick. 'You will take possession here one day,' she said to him, out loud, 'but not yet.'

Meanwhile she found she was bothered by the big stone altar. She draped a colourful tablecloth over it but that didn't seem to make any difference. Lachie had suggested she hold a dinner party around it to 'change the vibe', for what was an altar but a table in waiting? Soon she would have to find someone to remove it but for now she unpacked some cartons and piled it high with books: the Word camouflaged by words.

In the evenings she ate at her long, narrow dining table, like a monk in a refectory, gazing up at the image of Jesus surrounded by Roman soldiers on his way to Golgotha. Before she could do anything else, she first had to decide what to do with the windows. They would be expensive to remove and, even if she could afford to replace them, she feared that the installation of plain glass would make the interior resemble some kind of bland civic institution, like a mercantile town hall.

It was a Saturday morning and she was mowing the spiky yellow grass around the church with an old hand-mower. The grass was bone dry, a wheat colour, for the valley was in its fourth year of drought. She heard an engine, looked up and saw a black SUV crawl up the drive. It stopped in front of the porch and the driver stepped out, a ruddy, thickset man in tan boots, moleskins and a pale blue shirt. He introduced himself as Blair McAlister and, waving towards the electrified fence on the northern side, said he had the adjacent property. 'We're neighbours,' he said, and he wondered if he might have a word. 'There used to be something of interest here to my family.' He hadn't been in the church for a long time and he would be obliged if he could see if the item of interest was still there.

Inside, she offered him coffee, which he declined. There was something standoffish in his manner, a certain patrician reserve. 'Ah, there it is.' She followed his gaze to a brass plaque on the wall and they crossed the nave to look more closely, but already she knew what the plaque said.

SACRED TO THE MEMORY OF OUR DARLING SON
Lieut. Roy Angus McAlister
Killed on the Somme 21st August 1916
Aged 27
Forever in our hearts
He laid down his life for King and Country

'My great-grandfather's brother,' said McAlister, gazing up at the plaque with his bottom lip set firm. 'The eldest son. I was brought here to look at it when I was a boy, you know. It made quite an impression on me.' He turned to her, but did not look her in the eye, staring instead at the sunlit window behind her. 'It broke the old man. He had a stroke soon after and died.'

She waited, for she knew what he wanted.

'I wondered,' he began, 'if you had any plans…' He hesitated, looking around and gesturing at the plaques along both sides of the wall. 'Any plans for these.'

'Would you like it? Your plaque. You could take it now,' she offered.

'That's very good of you, most kind, but I won't trouble you today. These things can be quite hard to dislodge.' He produced a card from his breast pocket. 'Here's my number.' And then: 'With your permission, of course, I'll ask Mick Hanlon to come and collect it. Have you met Mick?' And he described a weatherboard cottage half a mile down the road from the church. 'Mick is one of my deer shooters, and when the church was a going concern he used to keep the grounds tidy. Cut the grass, kept the snakes at bay. A good fellow.'

He turned to leave, and then turned back. 'This land was granted to the church by my family.'

'I didn't know that.'

'Yes. For a long time the church was known locally as McAlister's Gift.'

'I see. That explains why it's so close to the pastureland.'

He nodded. 'Indeed.'

When McAlister had gone, she raised her eyebrows at Nick. *A going concern?* 'I think we've just been visited by the lord of the manor,' she murmured, and tucked McAlister's card into the fine gap between the plaque and the wall.

The following weekend, in a low mood and in need of company, she walked along the road, down to the timber cottage where Mick Hanlon lived. Hanlon answered the door and, before she could open her mouth, said, 'Oh, yes, been expecting you. Come in.'

The kitchen was a big room at the back that looked out onto a yard of sheds in various states of disrepair and the biggest chook run she had ever seen. There were also geese, and two donkeys in an adjacent paddock. Hanlon introduced his wife, Berenice, an attractive middle-aged blonde in tight jeans and a loose pink shirt unbuttoned at the top to reveal a deep cleavage. 'Bought the church then, did ya,' she said, with a knowing grin, as if they were old acquaintances sharing a joke. 'McAlister got you running around for him, has he?'

'Shush, Bern,' said her husband. 'Get you a drink, Zoe?'

'Thanks.'

'Beer?'

'That would be good.'

They settled at the table and it occurred to her that

the Hanlons were unlikely, either of them, to have been parishioners of St Martin's, or to know anything about its history or whether it had been deconsecrated. But she was wrong.

'My mum, Viv, she was very involved in it,' Mick said. 'Went to church every Sunday without fail. The bishop was supposed to come down for the big farewell and she organised the afternoon tea. Had the trestle tables set up outside, the white cloths, the lot. But he didn't front.'

'The bishop?'

'Yeah, didn't turn up. Must have got the dates mixed up. The Reverend Carter removed all the sacred objects, like, and they packed 'em up, the candlesticks and that, and he took 'em away, put 'em in a safe place somewhere. And that was that. We sat around on the fold-up chairs and ate the scones and the wasps got stuck into Viv's jam.'

Berenice rolled her eyes and shot Zoe a knowing look: *a fiasco*, it said.

'Where is Reverend Carter now?' she asked. 'I suppose they moved him to another parish.'

'No,' said Mick. 'Racked his cue. Bought a small farm on the other side of town and grows garlic. The purple stuff that costs a bomb. Ethiopian, or somewhere like that. Lovely bloke. Still does weddings and funerals if you ask, but obviously not in the old church. Bern's cousin's son passed last week and the Rev's conducting the funeral next Saturday at the Silver Wattle vineyard.'

Berenice sat with her chin resting on her left hand,

eyeing Zoe in a direct, appraising way. She leaned across the table, the bronze flesh of her bosom more exposed than ever. 'Why don't you come along and meet him?' she said. 'At the wake. He'd be interested to know who's in the old church.'

The invitation had an unexpected—a frank—intimacy. 'But I didn't know your nephew. I wouldn't want to intrude.'

'No-one'll mind that. You can meet some of the locals.'

She couldn't think of how to decline. They had been so open, so friendly, when they might have been wary and defensive. To change the subject, she raised the question of the plaque. She could understand the McAlister family wanting it. She knew that a lot of young men in regional towns had enlisted, a higher proportion than in the cities, and so many of them didn't come back.

Berenice gave her a look. 'Mmm…' She paused and leaned into the table. 'There's wars and there's wars, isn't there?' At which point Mick shot his wife a warning glance, but she ignored him. 'Old McAlister, he was the one, that fella, rounded up all the blackfellas on his property into a paddock—before the war, this is, the first one, the one they're grizzling about—set fire to the paddock and put his men all around it so the blackfellas couldn't get away.'

'Shush, Bern,' said Mick, and this time his tone was more threatening. He turned to Zoe. 'She's got a bit of the local blood in her,' he said, apologetically, 'and it rankles.'

Zoe froze. The heat in the kitchen was oppressive but a vein of ice water ran down her spine. The image of a burning paddock flared in her head, the dark silhouettes of figures ghosting in the smoke, flames lapping at the altar wall of the church. 'Good God!' she said, and it came out as a whisper.

Now a humid cloud hung in the room, hung so damp and heavy she could feel the weight of it press down against the thickness of her hair. At last, to fill the silence, she asked if there was a history of the valley that she could read.

'Well, that wouldn't be in it for a start,' said Berenice, who seemed quickly to recover her good humour, in a way that suggested she had never lost it, or her self-possession.

'No, I suppose not.' There was nothing else to say, at least not then. She drained her glass and got up to leave. 'Well, thank you both.'

But it was to Berenice that she addressed her words and the woman rose and followed her down the hallway. At the door Berenice tilted her head, still giving her shrewd, appraising look. 'You like deer?' she asked.

'I've never tried it.'

'Give you some if you like. Next time Mick brings home a kill.'

'You'll have to show me how to cook it.'

'Nothing to it. Just a long, slow simmer. Bit of red wine. Plenty of spice.'

Zoe smiled and nodded. The breath caught in her chest.

Along the road there was no walking path, only a rocky verge beside the electrified fence that lined the McAlister grazing lands. As she approached the church door, breathing heavily, she looked over to the rear paddock where the sheep stood motionless in the shade of an old cypress.

11

One night, restless from the heat and unable to sleep, she got up. She would make a cup of tea and read. After an hour she would go back to bed and set the alarm and, in any case, these days she seemed able to do without much sleep.

At the altar she removed the dust cover and chose a book, an old favourite, but once she had settled in an armchair, she soon found that the story had lost its power to compel her and the words slithered on the page like loose scrawls of ink. She was marking time, living like a squatter, aimless.

She laid the book aside and returned to the altar to search behind the reredos where Lachie had stacked boxes of her papers: correspondence, tax files, the many items she would need at some future date when she had completed her renovation and created a discrete nook for a filing cabinet.

She was looking for a box of Nick's papers she had kept, for after he had discovered the church online he had begun to think seriously about design options, and to calculate costs. Where would they begin? What might be the unforeseen pitfalls? From time to time he would raise the subject anew: 'You know, I've been thinking, if we bought that little church…'

The dust behind the reredos made her sneeze but she was able quickly to locate this box because Nick had marked it clearly with a thick black texta: THE CONVERSION. It wasn't heavy and she carried it across to the couch and set it down on the coffee table, where she cut the packing tape with scissors. On top of a messy pile of papers was a manila file, notes he had begun to make, and the sight of his hand-writing, bold and looping on sheets of thin, unlined paper, brought on a brief flush of tears. She put the file down and gazed for a while at the window opposite, where the rich crimson and gold of the apostles' cloaks had darkened into sombre shades of purple and bronze, and a crescent moon could be glimpsed above their heads.

When she opened the file, at first the words blurred in a haze, but after a while she began to make sense of what Nick had written. She had expected to find calculations and costs but instead found a sheaf of summary notes from a book Neville Glass had found at a Lifeline book sale, Mircea Eliade's *The Sacred and the Profane*. 'Here's some prep for you,' he had said, and she recalls how provoked she had been by Neville continuing to encourage Nick when he knew of her disapproval. Nick had said nothing to her about the book but clearly it had made an impres-sion on him, for here were his notes, with some phrases heavily underlined.

The world of secular or profane space is a chaos, lacking in a fixed point of orientation. It has no meaning other than what we bestow on it...

Unbuilt, undeveloped space is formless, a chaos of fragments. A surveyor can measure and cut it in any direction...

Both the temple and the church are a fixed point of orientation in a chaos of relative space. Without such a fixed point we have no reliable model of what is real, of objective reality...

We invent a meaningful cosmos to give it a form...We tell ourselves a creation story and enshrine it on an altar...

The church then is an orderly cosmos such as is needed to deliver us from the murk of the subjective, from the swamp of our disorientation, our unregulated desires. It is a fixed point where reality can make sense and the gods can be recognised...

On the one side of the thresholds there is a meaningful cosmos, on the other the chaos of a fragmented universe and the terror of the formless...

But then, at the bottom of the page, Nick had scrawled: 'Isn't all space sacred to someone? Do we need bricks and mortar?' And: 'This is a theory based on fear!'

It sounded so like him, so much so that he might

almost have been at her shoulder, and again the letters began to swim on the page, fissures in her sightline. It was too much. She stood abruptly, and for a moment was dizzy and dropped the file, the notes spilling onto the rug.

Steadying herself against the coffee table, she knelt to gather them and saw that among the larger pages there were some smaller ones, in Nick's hand, obviously a letter. It began, 'My darling girl…'

She gave a hoarse cry. My God, was there to be no escape? Was she to be haunted, even here? Leaving the pages scattered on the floor, she sank back onto the couch, and there the sickly fog enveloped her, the fog of *that room*.

Another Saturday afternoon, and she had arrived home in a good mood after buying herself a silk dress. The house was quiet, but something in her sensed a presence. 'Nick?' she called. No answer, but already she knew. No-one in the living room, so where?

From room to room she walked, in a soft, almost tentative tread, until she reached the small, claustrophobic room in the south-eastern corner of the house, the only room that they had neglected to renovate, perhaps because it was so dark. And there she was, on the floor, on the old carpet beside the shabby velvet curtains that smelled of mould. In the corner, in an abject crouch, the foetus, her delicate head resting against the embossed wallpaper. Nick was sitting on the floor, his back against the end of the single bed, waiting.

But this time, Zoe would not wait. 'Get up, Sophie,'

she snapped. How could Nick tolerate this? She turned to him, and he frowned at her and shook his head.

Fuming, she left them to it and went out into the front garden. The girl's bike was parked just inside their front gate, and she resisted an urge to push it over. Nick will fix this, she told herself, he had better—*this must be the last time*—and she opened the gate and in a furious stride made for the park opposite.

When she returned, the girl was gone. Nick was in the kitchen, rinsing a coffee mug. 'Are you in control of this or not?' she demanded.

'Almost,' he said, wearily. 'It won't be long.'

'We can't be her parents.'

'I know that, Zoe. And I've told her so.'

'She has no boundaries.'

'And that's why, next week, I'm going to use the walking therapy on her.'

'Good,' she said, 'not before time.'

The walking therapy was a technique he prided himself on, a weapon of last resort. It was something he had learned years ago at a seminar in San Francisco, and he had adapted it to his own theory about the individual's relationship to the space they inhabited, both physically and mentally. Wherever he had rooms for his practice he needed a large one, and this meant an expensive rental.

Holding the client gently by the shoulders (controversial, this—the human touch), he walked them around the room in a preordained pattern. And this continued for an hour. If the client was locked in an obsession, Nick believed it to be the equivalent of being locked in a very small attic room, an ever-shrinking room in which the walls came in until all that occupied the space was the obsession. The treatment, then, was to get them out of the psychic attic room into a larger space, both actual and symbolic, with him supporting their body, which might be limp, or rigid with resistance. It was a therapy of monotonous but ceremonial repetition, the walking, and the quiet reassurance of his voice if they faltered: 'Now turn around. Thank you.' And sometimes they threw themselves on the floor in an hysterical paroxysm, but rarely. The process grounded them, he said, and brought them into the present, both in space and in time.

It was especially effective if they were obsessing about something in their past, and since everything up until then was 'past' it relieved them of the burden of that past, a past that more often than not was annulled in the ritual monotony of the walking. When you are sitting in a chair and talking, you are locked in time, usually a time of trauma, and you relive it, and to what purpose? The walking was a technique for dissolving fixation, at least temporarily. It demanded an iron resolve from the therapist, and immense patience.

Problematical space is either too small and claustrophobic, or too big and amorphous. In the first instance the sufferer is locked in, in the second they bleed out into a chaos where they can't psychically find their feet, and it was a question of finding the right boundaries: the security of enclosure with freedom to move, spaciousness combined with intimacy. It rarely failed.

The night of the letter was long and she could not bear to remain inside. Wide awake in a pool of light from the tall reading lamp, she could smell that little room, and the girl in it, her musky perfume, the dusty carpet, threadbare where she crouched, like a cowering animal, the loops and swirls of the frantic wallpaper, the worn nap of the green velvet curtains, the smears of greasy dust on the window, and all of that dank Saturday afternoon when she had first opened the front door and chaos had entered her cosmos.

The smell of the girl, of the house she had lost, was overwhelming. Taking her biggest torch, she unbolted the door of the vestibule and strode out into the night, and began to walk the grounds of the church, around and around, eyes down and fixed on the yellow cone of light that flared ahead of her until, at last, a dry, hot northerly sprang up and she was driven back inside. She undressed and gulped down a sleeping pill.

In the morning she woke in a state of agitation. She could not eat, could not even face her coffee. She needed to take off, to go somewhere and leave the church to its ghosts. She needed to be among people, preferably in a crowd. The Silver Wattle vineyard. The funeral of Berenice Hanlon's nephew. No-one would notice her, and the presence of death, of someone else's suffering, would restore her sanity.

She had had no intention of gatecrashing a stranger's funeral but now, without any further thought, she found herself driving towards the vineyard.

The vines grew on a series of mellow slopes, at the top of which stood a semicircle of wooden chalets beside a function centre, open to the air but covered with a pitched roof that had a finial carved in the shape of a cluster of grapes. On the lawn outside, the deep green of artificial turf, a crowd was gathered in front of a dais with a microphone on a stand beside a table laden with flowers. There was no coffin in sight.

Only minutes after she arrived she saw Mick Hanlon mount the dais and call for quiet. Music began to ooze out of the speaker system and it sounded vaguely familiar, some kind of melancholy rock. The music died and Mick Hanlon stepped back up to the microphone and introduced the Reverend Patrick Carter, a tall, lean man in his sixties with grey hair and a trim grey beard. Dressed casually in jeans and a navy poloneck sweater, he looked like a fisherman. So this was the former vicar of St Martin's.

At the sight of Carter she felt relieved to be there. How odd, she thought. There was nothing about Carter that might be expected to bring on this feeling; perhaps it was the good-natured crowd, for those present seemed to exude a quietly festive air. It did not, she told herself, feel like a funeral.

Given the informality of the former vicar's dress, she

wondered what kind of eulogy he might have tailored for the occasion. And why him? Why not a civil celebrant? She assumed that he had become popular in the district and was preferred for that reason; he had been around a long time and they were used to him. But as she listened to Carter's words float out over the crowd, she began to think that there was more to it than mere familiarity.

The dead man, Brayden Madden, had been a commando and served three tours of duty in Afghanistan, and Carter began by saying that Brayden had served his country faithfully, that as a soldier he had been at the frontier of the horrors of the world and this had affected him profoundly. But he did not dwell on the war and moved on to speak of the dead man having started his working life in the coalmines before he joined the army, and how he came from a respected family of miners that had been in the valley for generations. In simple terms he evoked the labour of working underground, within the earth, the earth that made us, the earth that willingly takes us back, like a beloved who knows where our true home is, the earth that binds us together under a common sky. It might have sounded trite but in Carter's quiet, almost hesitant delivery it sounded like a revelation, newly and painfully arrived at.

The mourners were enjoined to bow their heads and contemplate the body that had left them while the spirit of the deceased remained in their hearts. We may have lingering grievances against the deceased and if so now was the time to surrender them, so that we could walk away in good faith, having made our peace and celebrated our common humanity. We are all at times tempted to see the world as broken, but the light of the world shines on regardless and that light is always within us.

There was no mention of God, or that the dead man had driven out into the bush and shot himself. This Zoe had learned from Karen Veitch, one of the nurses at the hospital. Brayden Madden had spent too much time in a bad place and it had 'got into his head', and so, as Karen put it, 'he ended it'.

Were priests allowed to officiate at the funeral of a suicide? Perhaps it was up to the priest. Perhaps it was okay so long as the priest was there in an unconsecrated location, such as a vineyard, and the name of God was not invoked. In that case, why ask him? In calling on Patrick Carter, did the community experience residues of faith, a filter through which an old notion of grace could pass without dark judgement and the invocation of sin? But how did Patrick Carter feel about that, she wondered. Was bringing comfort enough, an end in itself?

From a distance she spotted Berenice Hanlon, who just then turned and beckoned her to approach. But she did not want to join the wake. The others might not mind but to her it felt presumptuous, and she shook her head and pointed at her watch, feigning an appointment, and began to stroll down the hill towards her car while the music started up again, growing progressively fainter until she reached the bottom of the drive.

When she returned to the church the vault of space above her head was blessedly empty. Abandoned, left with nothing to feed on, the ghost had departed.

12

At the end of the month Neville Glass came to visit. 'There's no curtain over the shower,' she told him, and he gave his hoarse, guttural laugh. 'As long as I don't have to piss in the font,' he said.

He arrived in the late afternoon, climbing out of his car with all the gangly awkwardness of the very tall man he was. He kissed her brightly on both cheeks and patted her on the head as if she were a child and he an indulgent uncle. Then he beamed up at the belltower. 'What! No bell?'

'Too expensive.'

'What if there's a bushfire? You could alert the valley.'

'Yes, Nev.'

'It's a schizophrenic place, your little valley, isn't it? Half coalmines, half vineyards. You know, Zo, this valley has always had a weird feel to me. There's a darkness here.'

'It's called coal, Nev.'

He set his bags down on the dining table and began to unpack the food he had brought. With his customary generosity he had a carton of wine and two bottles of boutique gin ('wonderful botanicals'), chocolates, smoked eel, roast quail and a cloth bag of cheeses. She made them a gin and tonic and then, glasses in hand, gave him the tour.

'Ridiculously cheap,' he kept saying, 'they practically gave it away. The council could have bought this,' he added, 'would have a made a good community and function centre.' They already had one in the town, she pointed out. 'Yes, I drove past it, and it's shabby. Bad for local morale, I would have thought.'

'Well, they could renovate it, rather than buy a money pit like this.'

'Is it a money pit?'

'Not for me, but it would be for them. Think of the liability insurance. And besides,' she gestured at the stained-glass images that dwarfed them. 'The windows.'

'They are a bit overpowering, aren't they?' He looked up and smiled. 'My father would have hated them, old Calvinist that he was, you know, the human heart is a perpetual factory of idols.'

'He said that?'

'No, Calvin did.'

'That's rather good. But no help to me. I don't know what to do with them.'

'You'll have to do something. They're just single glass, so in winter they'll leak air unless they're reset and that would be costly. But anyway, you don't want them.' He shrugged. 'But you could put another layer of glass over them on the inside and make them double-glazed or double-panelled.'

'Also expensive. And I feel I can't solve any other problem until I solve this one.'

'So, who was your St Martin?'

She pointed to the figure in the metal breastplate and plumed helmet. 'A Roman soldier. Famous for being the first recorded conscientious objector.'

'Not a good career move for a Roman.'

'When they accused him of cowardice he offered to go into battle unarmed.'

'Died young, then.'

'No, the enemy signed a truce. He ended up a bishop.'

Again, the gasping laugh. 'Of course he did.'

'Cynic. I've grown rather fond of him.'

She set out the food he had brought and they sat at the long table and gnawed at their tiny birds. 'How are you, Nev?'

He sat with one long leg twisted around the other, his shoulders slumped forward, and grimaced. For the first time she saw that he was in a funk, the jovial energy of his arrival, his hypermanic bonhomie dissipating in the crystal alchemy of the gin. The medicinal botanicals were failing him. If Nick had been with them he would have been able to lift Neville's spirits; Nick had a way of making people feel more at ease in the world.

'How is your work going?'

'Oh, the usual. A war of attrition. Small gains. Some public space here, an avenue of trees there. But what a little island you have here. Things were looking so grim for you but now you have this.' He looked up and around him. 'It's like a sailing ship at anchor.'

'Except that now I'm here I'm beginning to see that I can't afford to convert it. I'm just camping, really.'

'But you seem happy.'

'I'm not unhappy.'

He looked around. 'What would you do if you had the money?'

'I don't know.'

'A mezzanine?'

'They give me vertigo.'

'What then?'

'Everything is so…so out of proportion.'

'Well, that's the thing with these conversions, you've got a problem of scale. But, you know, you could rig up a series of flexible partitions. I've seen it done in office space. They swing on hinges so that you create rooms.'

'How would that work?'

He looked up. 'You set up a kind of railing system suspended from the ceiling. You could use Japanese screens hanging from rails that could be adjusted to define spaces.'

'I think I need a project manager. Are you up for it?'

He knew she wasn't serious.

She cleared the dishes while Neville gravitated towards the pulpit. Boyishly he bounded up its stairs and threw his long, thin arms out wide. 'I come to bury Caesar, not to praise him…' He waited for the echo that didn't come, and then: 'The acoustics are good. Very good, actually. But you'd expect that. What are you going to do with the pulpit?'

'I don't know. I feel I should get rid of the altar first.' And she told him of how in many conversions the place where the altar stood had been filled with the marital bed.

'How very appropriate. The marital sacrifice replaces the Eucharist.' Neville was twice divorced and nurtured a certain bitterness.

She ignored this, pointed to her own altar and remarked on how even that was not adequate to the space, too low in relation to the vault of the ceiling, and this no doubt was the reason for the many reredos screens that were extravagantly tall and ornate, in order to bridge the space between earth and heaven. The simple table of the Last Supper, which the early Christians most likely set up in domestic homes, was now, in many larger spaces, not grand enough. It accounted, perhaps, for the desire of reformers to move the altar to the centre of the nave, where in any case it was still too small and, if the photos online were any indication, it could look a bit lost. The Gospels were nothing if not domestic, the churches anything but.

'You've really been thinking about this, haven't you?'

'Don't be patronising, Nev, of course I have.' She winced inwardly at her sharp tone. 'C'mon, I'll make us some coffee.'

When they were settled on the couch she said how pleased she was to see him, and that if she seemed on edge it was because she felt at sea. 'I suspect that whatever I might do, it would feel as if I were bending something out of shape.'

'That's superstition, Zo.'

'Yes, probably. Any ideas? You're the planner.' What had he learned from studying with Christopher Alexander? And could any of that be applied to St Martin's?

'Maybe. Maybe not. Alexander got lost in woolly metaphysics. Started off as a mathematician devising models. What's an ideal structure and how to create it?'

'Isn't that what all architects do?'

'Theoretically. But he came up with a wacky theory of how space works. Space, dear Zoe, is an abstraction, but Alexander believes that it's inherently alive—he's a sort of mad Catholic—and if you can get all the parts to create a satisfying whole you release its latent energy. A good space has what he calls a quality without a name, something you feel as soon as you enter it. You feel happier, more your-self, the effect that any public space all too rarely has.'

'So you agree with him?'

'In practical terms, but only up to a point. He has some sensible things to say about proportion, symmetry, boundaries in the right place, meaningful ornament, that sort of thing.'

'I don't see how that's different from what other people say.'

'Well, that's where it gets woolly. You can treat space

in such a way as to deaden its aliveness or draw it out, and to do that you have to create strong centres. And now you're going to ask me what a strong centre is.'

'Yes.'

'A part within the whole that has its own strong field of energy that resonates with other centres that make up the whole.'

'Like an altar?'

'Well, maybe. Depends on how the altar is configured.'

'So it's a matter of taste.'

'No, it's more about coherence. Take this place,' he looked around him. 'Like it or not, it has a coherence. Everything relates harmoniously to everything else: the font, the pulpit, the altar, the windows. Alexander would call them strong centres that make up a whole greater than the sum of its parts. Remove one of the elements and you diminish the others.'

'Of meaning?'

'Not exactly—of energy. This is the woolly bit. Energetically, if you like, the church is all of a piece, a unified field. Except for your vestibule, which is bare and gives you away.'

'Gives me away?'

'Yes. Empty. Unloved. It shows you are at sixes and sevens. Without a plan.' He leaned towards her intently. 'As an atheist, you now have the problem, dear Zoe, of producing the same degree of coherence in a different form.'

'So I have to create my own centres? Or something like that.'

'You already have one.' He nodded in the direction of the sideboard. 'And look, you've set it up in opposition to the altar. You've made a start. And the table here. The flowers at the centre, the fruit bowl.' He shrugged. 'Lovely. Alexander would say that you've brought the space above the table alive.' He stretched out his long legs and flexed his shoulders. 'I'm stiff,' he said. 'I'm not getting enough exercise.' *She's putting up a good front, a brave face for now, and I'll play along with it. I won't bring up the subject of Nick—I'll wait for her to do it. In her own time.*

'We can go for a walk if you like.' It was a warm night and still light.

'Where?'

'Oh, just in the grounds.'

He helped her to clear the table and they strolled out into the balmy softness of the evening. On the steps of the entrance she paused and pointed to the row of old pines. 'They're ugly,' she said, 'but they bring the black cocka-toos, so I'll keep them.'

'Just as well. Fearfully expensive to hire an arborist. And then you'd get the heritage people on your case.'

They began their walk along the boundaries of the churchyard, and she warned Neville of the electrified fence.

'There should be signs up,' he said.

'Not here. There are things in the country you are expected to know.'

The evening sky had clouded over, and as if on cue a trio of black cockatoos flew over their heads in a swooping glide. She was delighted and waved at them. Could it be that rain at last was coming? 'So often the clouds darkened and then moved on. 'See,' she said to Neville, 'they visit me,' and she took his arm, in the old-fashioned way.

They walked on down the driveway to close the gates that she had left open for his arrival, and on the verge she pointed across the road to the old graveyard. At that moment a black SUV slowed to a halt beside them, and Blair McAlister wound down his window.

'Mrs North,' he began. 'I've been meaning to thank you for the plaque.'

Mick Hanlon had come one evening on his way home and removed it.

'No trouble at all. Mick was very quick about it.'

'I'm thinking about where to put it. Quite an interesting question.'

'I suppose it is.' There was a pause. She felt he wanted to go on with the conversation but she gave him no encouragement. Beside him, in the passenger seat, was a young woman who did not acknowledge them but looked fixedly ahead with a sour expression. His daughter, perhaps. They had the same reddish-brown hair.

The silence was awkward. 'Very dry around here,' Neville offered. 'How are you getting on?'

'Worst drought in thirty years. I've had to sell stock.'

Zoe looked up and into the distance, as if something there had caught her attention. McAlister took the hint and bade them goodnight.

'Who was that?' asked Neville after McAlister had driven off.

She explained.

'Snooty little piece next to him.'

'I didn't notice.' She had.

'I thought *he* looked at you in a certain way.'

'Don't be ridiculous.'

They walked back up the drive in silence, with Neville now in a sombre mood. At the big door he paused and sighed heavily. Inside he slumped onto the couch while she poured them another drink. 'I miss your old man,' he said.

'We all do.'

She had no desire to talk about Nick and thought she had done a good job of distracting Neville by asking him about Christopher Alexander. She stood and moved across to the sideboard, busied herself opening cupboards and pretended to look for the box of candles Lachie had given her when she knew exactly where they were. 'Here they are,' she said brightly, and set them down on the coffee table and lit them. 'Let's watch the late news,' she said, and turned out all the lights but for the two floor lamps.

They settled back on the long couch and before long a light breeze began to waft in through the leaky windows and from under the door, so that the candle flames flickered in unison and the church itself seemed to palpitate. Before long Neville was dozing on the couch and emitting a light snore, and she sat and contemplated his narrow, angular head thrown back against the rim of the cushioned leather, half in shadow. Her oldest friend. And then he woke and shook his head. 'Sorry,' he said. 'Too much of the local brew.'

She pointed to one of the army cots that she had bought from the disposal store in the hope that her grandchildren would visit her at Easter. 'I'm afraid your feet will dangle over the end.'

But he smiled and patted her on the arm. 'I'm so tired I could sleep on a stone ledge.'

In the night she woke. She could hear Neville groaning and wondered if he was having a nightmare. But then her ears became accustomed to the rhythmic squeaking of the cot bed, and a sobbing kind of breath, an anguished, gasping sound.

In the morning she teased him over breakfast. 'Neville, were you wanking last night?'

'Sorry, did I wake you?'

'You were moaning.'

'It was the windows.'

'*The windows?* In the dark?'

'The light was coming in from the moon. It was lovely. Like a micro-dose of acid.' He sat back in his chair and gave his choking laugh. 'Suddenly I felt *good*!' Then he sighed and was grave. 'I haven't felt good in ages.'

After some toast and coffee they went for another stroll around the grounds, and when they returned Neville packed his bag. In the vestibule he gave her one of his awkward, bony hugs. 'I see that you're okay,' he said.

'Yes. Yes, I am.'

'Let me know if you want to chew over your future plans.'

'I'm in no hurry.'

'I see that.'

She waved him off from the door. And felt grateful for his visit. With his own quirky brand of tact he had made only the one brief reference to Nick, had offered her an opening to speak of him but had sensed her resistance and not pressed it. But his presence had raised the ghost.

There had been one more episode. They were both at home, and the girl came to the back door that was open to the winter sun and hovered there under the lintel. Nick was in his workshop, and Zoe, speechless with anger, turned her back to gather her thoughts, and began to clear the table which was still strewn with the remnants of lunch. When she turned around she found that, soundlessly, the girl had disappeared. Good, she thought, she's got the message and gone. Then she heard a quiet keening coming from down the hallway and felt sick in the pit of her stomach. *Not again.* She found her, this time in their own bedroom, in a corner, crouched on her haunches, her face raised upwards, her eyes closed, a low wail issuing from her open mouth.

Without a word she strode down the hallway and out into the workshop where Nick was sharpening the gardening shears. 'She's back!' she hissed. 'Deal with it!' And he glared at her and strode off into the house and into the bedroom where, in one swift movement, he seized hold of the girl and yanked her to her feet. 'Go, Sophie!' he said, his face in a tight grimace. 'Go now!' But she twisted away from him and collapsed onto the bed so that he leaned over and, clutching her from behind, with his arms under her breasts, hoisted her up, though she fell back against his chest like a rag doll. It was ugly. But he was not deterred and, grasping her firmly by one arm, he dragged her into the hall, and gathering up her helmet in his other hand steered her towards the front door, wrenched it open and pushed her through, slamming it shut.

Then he turned to Zoe and glared again. 'Don't say a word,' he said. 'Not a single word.'

She stood there, stunned at the familiar way in which he had manhandled the girl. She should have known then.

It was not long after this that she became aware that he had stopped talking about the church. She wondered at this but thought she would let sleeping dogs lie. He seemed more cheerful.

'Are you still seeing that girl?' she asked one evening. (Why did she ask? She never asked.)

Nick had been working on accounts at the kitchen

table. In the soft light, with his hair rumpled, his white shirt open at the collar and sleeves rolled to the elbow he looked like a younger man, with a muscular alertness in his body that he had when he was content.

'Yes,' he said, and went on working.

'Still depressed?'

'Not exactly.'

He seemed not to want to talk about it but she persisted. 'Then what?'

He put down his pen and folded his arms across his chest. Such beautiful forearms: they had always affected her, in the way that a single feature can bind you to another's body.

'She feels empty. She says she is a vacant space, there is a hole at her centre. She's had boyfriends but in sex she feels nothing, only that any boyfriend she has is thrusting into a black hole.'

'She's frigid?'

'That's a discredited idea, Zo. No-one is frigid.'

He was telling her that she shouldn't have asked and it provoked her. She had had to put up with this interloper so she was entitled to an explanation. But he rose from the table and said that he felt like a walk. He had been stuck in stuffy rooms all day and needed some fresh air. He put on his jacket and left.

The house felt empty; not in the usual way when she was alone in it but uncannily, as if something or someone had departed who was never coming back.

13

She was grateful for her work at the hospital, and it was not just the modest salary. There were hours when she forgot herself, and the relief of this was a blessing. Compared to her past life, relatively little was demanded of her and yet she felt useful.

It was a Thursday morning, and just before lunch a young woman stumbled into the reception area with agonising stomach cramps. She leaned against the counter and could barely stand. Zoe pressed the buzzer on the desk and ran around to the other side where she attempted to hold the woman up, but she was heavy, and seeing this an elderly man got up from one of the couches and helped her guide the woman along the passage to the emergency room. Her face was contorted, tears streaked the dirt on her cheek and she had vomited onto her steel-capped workboots. Her navy work clothes and hi-vis vest were dishevelled and her hair smelled of diesel.

Just before they reached the entrance to the emergency room she doubled over in a sudden lurch forward and vomited onto Zoe's sneakers. 'I'm so sorry,' she gasped, her eyes filling with tears, 'so sorry.'

Zoe squeezed her arm. 'It's not important,' she said, steering her towards the surgical bed where the young nurse's aide, Caitlin, helped to hoist her onto the crisp white sheet and then gently removed her boots.

'It's all right, Leanne,' Caitlin said, 'doctor's coming.'

Four hours later Leanne was delivered of a baby girl, to her amazement and that of her husband, Sean, a lanky labourer from one of the local vineyards who barely arrived in time to witness the miracle. Leanne and Sean had no idea they were pregnant. There had been no morning sickness, no cessation of periods, no movement in the womb and at forty-one weeks this unknown and undeclared sprite had decided to emerge in every way unannounced, the mother stunned, the father barely unable to contain his elation, clasping his tattooed arms around his trunk and exclaiming, over and over, 'What about that! *What about that!*'

She had heard of the phenomenon when she was a trainee. A stealth pregnancy, they called it, which had struck her as too sinister a name, as if the child were a hi-tech bomber that flew over defensive installations at night to ambush its targets in the dark. In some of the locals it was to provoke a derisive dismissal of the mother: how could she be such a cretin, so out of touch with her own body? Then again, she was a big woman and had put the added weight down to the stress of her job at the mine, driving a truck; often too tired in the evenings to cook, she had, in her words, eaten too much junk food.

Soon the event took on a festive character, and the response of the town moved from ridicule to celebration, as if an auspicious omen had appeared in the sky. There was a name day held at the community centre on a Sunday morning and a small crowd gathered outside on the lawn, presided over by a civil celebrant, Gail McVilly, she who was chair of the hospital board and had given Zoe her job. And hospital staff who had been in attendance that day were invited. Gail wore one of her flowing kaftans in orange and grey stripes, and presided with an easy but warm authority that reminded Zoe of one of the better magistrates.

After speeches by the father and Dr Khalid—whose presence, it was felt, was needed to certify the phenomenon—Gail asked the parents to come forward with the baby. 'We all love a good surprise,' she said, 'and this is about as good as it gets.' She asked the parents to lift her in the air, so that those assembled could christen the baby by shouting her name. 'We are now going to name this baby,' Gail declared, 'and on the count of three I want you to join me in shouting as loud as you can. Right, here we go. One, two, three…' And together they all shouted *Delta Rhiannon O'Dea!*, which produced prolonged cheers and whistling from the back, followed by a ripple of sheepish laughter. One of the older nurses, Yvonne, turned to Zoe and rolled her eyes: 'You see it all in this town.'

'I'd like to see more of it,' she said, and meant it, for the event had an atmosphere of the carnivalesque, a licensed rowdiness, both strange and hopeful, as if the mundane and besieged world could still surprise them all with the marvellous and the defiantly fertile. She thought of how, during Leanne's labour, she had removed her soiled sneakers, dropped them into a plastic bag and dumped them in one of the rubbish bins outside the hospital. That evening she had driven home in bare feet and felt uncommonly free.

14

It was a Saturday morning and she had not long been out of bed when there was a knock on the door of the vestibule.

She opened it to a man who looked like he might be in his early forties. He was short and scruffy, his fair hair falling onto the top of his glasses, and he wore a permanent grin of mischievous glee. 'Is this St John the Baptist's?' he asked.

'No, it's not anything now, but it used to be St Martin's.'

'Then I'm lost. I must have taken a wrong turn. Do you know where St John's is?'

'It's in the next town, Stoneybrook. This is Crannock. Have you got a phone?'

'Not a smart phone.'

'Then I'll draw you a map.' She invited him in and he looked around. 'You don't have an organ,' he observed.

'No.'

'Hmm, pity.'

She took in his worn sneakers, ill-fitting jeans and cheap short-sleeve shirt in a green-and-white check. In one back pocket was an unopened Mars Bar and in the other a half-empty bottle of Coke. He took her rough map, said thanks very much like a polite schoolboy, and she ushered him out. But within minutes he was back: his car wouldn't start. Did she have any jumper leads? No, she didn't. She rang the local garage that looked after her car and the young mechanic, Jason, said he could come out around noon and have a look. But that was two hours away.

'Oh dear,' said her visitor, who by now had introduced himself, at her prompting, as Colin Cross. 'I have to be back in town for a recital at five. I don't suppose you could give me a lift?'

A recital? Colin, it turned out, was an organist from the conservatorium. St John's had one of the oldest organs in the country and he wanted to play it. He had rung the vicar, who said he would leave the church unlocked until one in the afternoon and Colin was welcome to play the organ any time up until then.

Would she have been so accommodating if she had not been curious about the interior of St John's? In any case, they drove off and were soon there and she was glad she had come. Colin was clearly an adept, perched up in front of the great pipes like an eager schoolboy, filling the empty space with what he later told her was a Bach toccata, the sound of the organ crashing down around her head in bone-jarring chords.

Zoe was more interested in the windows, which could only be described as bizarre. On one side of the nave was an almost naked and life-size Christ, muscular and blond, immersed to the waist in water in the act of being baptised by a ferociously bearded and skeletal John the Baptist. And on the opposite wall stood the figure of Salome, her face set in a fierce grimace as a Roman soldier presented her with John's head on a gold platter. At her feet, the neck of John's decapitated body was leaching a pool of thick, dark blood.

How blunt and heavy the figures were, and she saw that they lacked the fineness of line and the luminous palette of the windows in St Martin's. For the first time it occurred to her that she was the beneficiary of a supe-rior artist. I could never live in this place, she thought, not even for a month, not where the maker of the glass had not been up to the challenge of transforming an obscene act into an image of the sacred. It was a failure of artistry; the horror had not been redeemed.

When Colin descended from the loft she pointed to the Salome window. He looked up, grinned and turned towards the door. The bottle of Coke in his back pocket was empty. In the vestibule he took it out and left it on the oak side-table next to a brass bowl of yellow and pink dahlias, the tips of their fine petals beginning to turn brown. 'Your bottle,' she said, but he kept on walking. *Pagan*, she thought and left the bottle where it stood.

They climbed into the car and, as she slid the latch of her seatbelt into its metal mouth, she felt hollow, as if she were a puppet with an empty chest and a cloth head.

Where had this mood come from? It was the church: its ugliness, its brutal piety. This church was dark, its windows an insult to the senses. In a surly mood she drove Colin back to his car, making it clear she did not want to talk, and Colin was content to sit like an amiable child with a bland, smiling expression, as if he were a tourist on a day excursion, taking in the scenery.

As she pulled into the drive, Jason arrived and soon Colin was on his way. She on the other hand sat limply in a chair, feeling as if the air had been sucked out of her chest. What feeble play was this? She was drifting and at a loss. I am stalled, she thought: I have become a student of windows. Moreover, the realisation that her own windows were very fine, the work of a true artist, compounded the problem of what to do with them. But she must do something. *I must make a beginning or the ghost will never leave me.*

That night, in a spasm of self-reproach, she rang Mick Hanlon and asked him to come and advise on the removal of the altar. While she could not yet resolve the problem of the windows, she could at least begin with that cumbersome block of stone.

Mick was prompt. He turned up the following evening with Berenice, who handed Zoe a plastic bag with a solid hunk of dark red meat in it that sat in an even darker pool of blood.

'Deer,' she said. Then she pulled a piece of neatly

folded paper out of her bosom. 'There's your recipe.'

Zoe thanked her and put the bag in the fridge.

'Still thinking about it, then?'

'What?'

'This place. Your renos.'

'Yes, and I need to get a move on.'

Berenice grinned and was about to say more but Mick interrupted. 'The font,' he said, gesturing at the hexagonal shape carved in stone that stood near the door to the vestibule. 'Any plans for that? Make a nice birdbath.'

'How would you remove it?'

'Been thinking about that. I'd bring in a Genie lift. You can hire one for a day, cost you around the two-hundred-dollar mark. Then you'd have a hole in the floor where the pipe is for the christening water to drain out, so you'd have to dig that out and replace the floorboards.'

'Is that something you could do?'

'Yeah, reckon I could. Be a day's work.'

'What about the altar?'

'Ah, more of a problem there. Might have to think about that. It's a big piece, that one.' He shook his head. 'Heavy. Mum always reckoned it was too big for a small church.'

Zoe might have known the altar would be a problem.

She offered Mick and Berenice a drink and the three of them sat outside on the camp chairs nursing their beers and looking out over the valley to where a full moon hung low above the coral rim of the dusky hills, the sky a painter's wash of uneven hues.

Mick began to talk about his plans for the future and of setting up an earthmoving business with his son, Travis. Travis was in his last year at school and didn't have many clues about what he wanted to do next. He wasn't a particularly practical kid—'bit of a dreamer,' this from Berenice—but Mick would train him up, give him a future. There was work Mick couldn't do on his own and, while he sometimes got his cousin in to help with the heavy lifting, Phil wasn't always available. And he didn't want Trav to go down the mine. Money was good but coal was on the way out, any fool could see that, and Mick liked to look ahead, to read the tea leaves. Get a lock on the future.

All the while Berenice sat looking out to the hills with her wry smile, occasionally adjusting the underwire of her bra that chafed beneath her breasts. When at last Mick paused in his ruminations, she turned to Zoe and winked. 'The future,' she said, 'where's that?'

15

Easter fell early in April, and in the third week of March Lachie rang: he would be visiting for Easter weekend and bringing the children. He had booked a camping site in the nearby national park and they could all camp together. Alice would not be coming because her triathlete event had been rescheduled and she had to fly to the Gold Coast.

This was news. Her daughter-in-law had begun by running half-marathons and this was the first Zoe had heard of an expansion in her ambition, but then Alice had always been a mystery to her. Did she run half-marathons by choice, or because she lacked the stamina for the other half? Zoe was curious but had never asked because the question might have implied judgment, or a probing for weakness. She liked Alice but they never seemed able to talk about anything for very long, not even the polite, animated chatter that women considerately dish out to one another as a form of civility and that men, wrongly, sneer at or dismiss.

She told Lachie about the two army cots she had bought for Isaac and Tess. He could sleep on the big couch.

And there was the deer, her gift of bleeding meat.

She would cook it for Lachie and then freeze it in batches because there was so much of it; she searched online for a recipe to match against the one Berenice had given her and they were almost identical. Red wine, rosemary, coriander and orange juice, all of it in a cast-iron casserole dish and three hours in a slow oven. The following evening she prepared it as soon as she arrived home and ate a late dinner, just a cup full of the meat and a salad. She froze the rest.

The next day she texted Mick: 'Please thank Berenice for the deer, it was delicious.' Mick texted back: 'Never mind Bern. I'm the one who shot it.'

When they arrived on Good Friday afternoon Lachie was uncharacteristically irritable. He looked around the church and sniffed the air. 'Honestly, Mum, this place needs vacuuming. So much dust. You know how it affects Isaac's asthma.'

'I vacuumed it yesterday.'

'You wouldn't think so.'

'You look tired, Lachie.'

'It's a long trip.'

'How were the children?'

'I bribed them. Hot chips and Queen on a loop.'

It was so long since she had seen the children and she could not take her eyes off them: the fineness of their skin, the sheen of their hair, their blithe loveliness that surprised her anew. It was their first visit and they wandered around in mild awe, staring up at the coloured glass. 'Why do you have pictures on your windows?' asked five-year-old Tess.

'Because it used to be a church.'

'What's a church?'

Where to begin? She decided this was not a conversation she wanted to have at this particular time and it might indeed be better left to their father, who ought to have prepared them.

'It's a place where people get married,' said nine-year-old Isaac. He turned to Zoe. 'I went to a wedding once, with Mum and Dad.'

Tess was gazing up at the figures in the stained glass: 'Who are those people?'

'That one is Jesus.' She pointed and was about to ask if Tess knew who Jesus was when Tess, looking solemn, piped up. 'My friend Sienna says that Jesus is her best friend.'

'He's dead,' Isaac said with the scorn of an older brother, 'he can't be your best friend.'

'He's not mine; he's Sienna's.'

And so her first theological conversation since moving into the church began with her grandchildren, whom, easily distracted, she ushered into the sacristy kitchen for pancakes.

In the late afternoon Lachie received an alert on his phone to say that there was a bushfire warning in the hills behind the national park and all bookings were cancelled. Neither of them was surprised: there had been a forest fire to the west of Crannock a month before, the land around them was tinder dry and they could detect the unmistakeable smell of eucalypt smoke. They promised the children a trip to the wildlife park north of Crannock as compensation and she set up a giant jigsaw she had bought for them, a map of the world with images of indigenous wildlife.

Lachie had stowed his camping gear behind the altar screen and he rummaged in one of the packs and produced a contraption that he wanted to show her. 'Gas is on the way out,' he said, 'better to use this.' *This* turned out to be a Biolite, and Lachie explained: 'Basically, you don't need any gas canister—you just need twigs and sticks, and really not that many. You have to feed it a bit but it gets hot quickly and boils things. The little fan makes the fire burn well and then the fire creates energy, which you can use to charge your phone.'

'Don't you go into the bush to get away from your phone?'

'It's a safety measure. Would you go out on a boat without a flare?'

The good son: always so careful, always so well prepared.

The children yawned through an early supper but came to life as she cleared the dishes. Lachie had bought them new head torches and they clamoured for an excursion to, in Isaac's words, 'test them out'. And so when it was almost dark Lachie and the children wandered around outside and looked for bugs while Zoe sat on the warm stone steps of the vestibule and watched as their narrow columns of light traced paths around the church-yard. Autumn. Too late for snakes.

Easter Saturday, and in the late morning they drove the children to the local animal park for rescued wildlife. Burnt koalas, wedge-tail eagles caught in wind-turbine blades, torpid snakes, rackety galahs, a scrawny emu that pecked ferociously at Lachie's hand while the children gave a half scream, half laugh, an albino wombat and indolent, overfed kangaroos lazing on the grass. There were two black swans in an enclosure beside a small pond, and as Lachie and Zoe ushered the children across a narrow wooden bridge that ran beside the enclosure the bigger of the two swans began to beat his powerful beak against the low wooden fence so that the planks shook, and the ferocious beating of the angry bird, so loud and so close, alarmed Tess.

They ate their sandwiches and ice-creams in the cafe and then drove ten minutes south to the abandoned church of St Stephen's, which Zoe wanted to show Lachie. Isaac and Tess were appeased for the duration of the drive by the gifts she had bought them in the wildlife shop but Lachie was dubious. 'Seriously, Mum, another church?'

'You're a history teacher. I think this will interest you.'

Like St Martin's, St Stephen's Anglican church stood on a low hill above the small settlement of Rianna, the site of an abandoned colliery and now just a handful of weather-board cottages occupied by farm and vineyard workers and a shabby general store. The stone church was a ruin, having burned in the infamous bushfire of 1932. Long neglected, its wooden roof had collapsed and some of its windows were boarded up where they had been vandalised, but what she wanted to show Lachie was a wooden plaque at the side of the church.

They climbed out of the car to breathe in the acrid smoke of the distant bushfire, just a whiff carried on a light breeze, and Isaac asked: 'Are we near the fire, Dad?'

'No, mate, nothing to worry about. It's a long way from here.'

She led them to the plaque that had been installed to showcase the significance of the stained-glass window above what had once been the altar. It had survived the fire but was now obscured not by an iron grille of the kind that protected St Martin's but by a sheet of mesh wire so fine and so encrusted with dirt that it obscured the figure in the glass. The plaque read:

> The window above St Stephen's altar is based on the famous painting *The Light of the World* by the Pre-Raphaelite painter William Holman Hunt (1827–1910). The figure of Jesus holds a lamp in the dark as he prepares to knock on an overgrown door. *Behold, I stand at the door and knock; if any man hear my voice, and open the door, I will come in to him, and will sup with him, and he with me.* REVELATION 3:20.

Lachie smiled and patted her on the shoulder. 'Are you jealous that you don't have a famous painting?'

'That's not why I brought you here. I thought you might be interested to know that a version of the Hunt painting—he did three of them—toured the world, around 1905 I think it was, and the biggest crowds were in Australia. Doesn't that surprise you? It did me. It's supposed to have been visited by four-fifths of the population. Imagine that. In Melbourne, people stampeded at the entrance to the exhibition hall. Inside, men removed their hats, people spoke in a whisper and some fainted. Millions of homes around the world had a copy hanging on the wall. I looked it up and it's been described as the first mass-produced image of the modern era. Now it's forgotten.'

'Are you getting nostalgic, Mum?'

'You can't get nostalgic for what you've never had. But it's an interesting reminder of just how much things have changed.'

'Yes, and for the better.'

All the while the children ran through the decrepit graveyard, dodging broken stone and trailing long stalks of dried grass, pausing to lash out at one another in mock swordplay. And she envied their innocent opportunism. Chips, Queen on a loop, some rubber snakes from the wildlife shop. And then she remembered: 'the light of the world'. She had heard that phrase before. Patrick Carter had inserted it into his eulogy at the funeral in the Silver

Wattle vineyard. A seed planted in the dark.

By then the smell of the smoke had grown more pungent. Her throat was dry and her sinuses stung.

'That smell is toxic,' she said to Lachie.

'You know, I've always liked it,' he said. 'As long as you're not too close.'

'Well, I think we're close enough for now.'

'Don't worry, Mum. It's a long way off.'

In the evening the children were lively and it took some time before they settled in their cots. Lachie was exhausted and, while he and the children slept, she trod soundlessly around the nave, hiding small Easter eggs in colourful foil wrappers: in the font, under the cushions on the couch, in the fruit bowl on the table, on the floor of the pulpit, on the altar, in and round the piles of books, and behind the altar screen. Beside the children's cots she placed a large chocolate rabbit in gold foil for Tess, and another in red foil for Isaac. Lachie was asleep on the couch, wrapped in his sleeping bag, and she stood for a moment and contemplated again that dear face, so like his father's. Then she got into bed and lay staring up at the cast-iron chandelier.

The moon beamed in from above the head of St Peter so that the furniture and fittings in the church were visible in shadowy outline, an ensemble of stately props from a cancelled performance, static ghosts in an old theatre. And yet she was content. The church had filled with her flesh and blood. For some time she lay there until, glancing at the phone beside her bed, she saw that it was just after midnight, the first minute of the day of Resurrection. And should she explain this to the children in the morning? And would ever it matter if they didn't know or understand? In the years to come they would most likely find their myth of redemption elsewhere.

Somewhere in that night she dreamed of a cathedral. Was it Cologne? It looked like it. Or, rather, it felt like it. Yes, it was Cologne cathedral. As a young woman she had caught only a glimpse of it when she and Nick sped past it on a train beside the Rhine but it had stunned her, the enormity of it, its spiky towers like black skeletons, its façade darkened by acid rain. For years after, it had lingered in her mind as the very image of Europe, dark, monumental Europe. And now in the dream she was once again on the train, this time with the children. 'Look,' she said, pointing out the window at the great mass of the cathedral. 'Look, there is the castle of God's stones.' But the children turned away and began to play with a naked doll that had appeared on the seat beside them. 'Where is Lachie?' she fretted. 'Where is he? The train will leave and he will be left behind.'

But the children were absorbed in their play, stroking the doll and trying to get it to drink from their plastic water bottle. With a jolt the train began to move from its platform while the cathedral remained behind: rearing, silent, empty, and yet somehow familiar as it had never been in life.

16

She had gone to stay with her sister, Isobel, in Newcastle and the weather had been foul. Heavy rain and strong winds, and they had got on each other's nerves. She had come home a day early and as she entered the house, in the early afternoon, she heard a bellowing noise coming from the living room. Instinct froze her and she trod softly like a thief to the open door, and there they were, the girl on her knees, naked between his thighs with his penis in her mouth, suckling like a pale but nimble calf. And Nick, his long, bony figure stretched out on the couch, legs splayed, arms spread wide, head thrust back, mouth agape, groaning like a wounded animal.

They were too absorbed to see her and she withdrew, stepping backwards, silently, all the way down the hall. The violence of the scene took her breath away. There was no tenderness in it, only a hungry, wounded desperation.

She left the house and sat on a bench in the park opposite and waited for the sound of the girl's bike, roaring off into the distance.

That night he sat at the kitchen table and wept. He had

tried the walking therapy and it hadn't worked. If only she hadn't resisted it. On the first morning that he had attempted it she had torn herself from his gentle hold and thrown herself onto the carpet, where she had begun to sob. 'Get up, Sophie,' he had said—this had never happened before—but when the sobbing exploded in an anguished wail, he had bent to grasp her by the hands so that he could pull her up from the floor, and with a sudden wrench she had twisted free of him and ripped open her shirt to expose her breasts. Stunned, he had knelt to grasp her shoulders and drag her to her feet but then he had looked into her sad, molten black eyes and in one deranged moment had bent to draw her right nipple into his mouth. And that was the beginning of the end.

'You old fool,' she said. 'She wanted a father, not a lover.'

'That's what *you* think.'

'That's what I know.'

'She was going to die. She was refusing to eat. I had to do something.' His voice came out in an anguished croak. And he began to sob and laid his head on the table. Then lifted his head and was calm. 'You can't imagine,' he said. 'Her need was so great. It was in its way perfect.'

How could he say this to her? And yet she knew, despite everything, what he meant. Of course it was. The girl's desperation had made it so. He had never felt so needed, needed in every muscle and bone, every pore.

And was her own soul so corrupt that she should comprehend this?

She stood behind him and might have struck him but instead put her arms around his shoulders and they wept together.

He slept in one of the spare bedrooms and in the morning he packed a small suitcase and moved into a motel a block down the road. She searched in the bathroom cupboard for some Valium she had been prescribed once when she had hurt her back. It was out of date but potent enough to put her in a manageable haze while she got through the next few days.

And then she received a note from the girl. 'You must help me,' she wrote. 'He is eating me alive.'

That night Zoe rang and invited him to dinner.

She set the table carefully and kissed him lightly when he arrived. She could see he was exhausted, and his eyes were bloodshot. He sat at the kitchen table and she poured him a drink, and while he sat, fingering the stem of his glass, she got a plate out of the cupboard, placed the girl's note on it and set it down in front of him.

'Congratulations,' she said.

He glanced down at the note and turned grey, then looked up and glared at her. 'You have no idea. *No idea!*' His mouth sagged open and he raised his fists in the air, not at her but at some phantom adversary. He stood and flung back the chair so that it fell to the floor with a sharp crack. Then he strode down the hallway to the front door.

That night, on his way to Sophie, his heart failed him. In the midst of a seizure on a steep incline—there were witnesses—he drove into a telegraph pole with such force that the wood snapped in half.

17

At the funeral there were many mourners. Zoe had wanted a private service but for once Lachie asserted himself against her and put a public notice in the paper. The number of cards and notes she received was beyond reckoning.

Neville Glass delivered the eulogy but the words were like puffs of cottonwool that floated across her sight line. She was affronted by the banality of the funeral home and the two giant white urns filled with fake Christmas lilies: waxy white blooms framed by rubbery green monstera leaves and coils of foliage made of something that looked like black wire. Nick would have hated it. In the front row of glossy white chairs trimmed with gilt paint and padded in scarlet upholstery, she sat woodenly next to her two sons, while Lachie wept silently and Dominic stared blankly ahead.

Dom had flown up for the day—'I can't stay'—and at the sight of him her knees had buckled and she thought she might faint. He had put his arms around her and she had felt the tension in his wasted body but said not a word. She would not reproach him. One day he would be better.

And he had embraced his brother, which was something. Looking at them, seated side by side, she could see that their bodies inhabited a space that they alone shared, that their intimacy was undiminished. This was her consolation: if they could continue to love one another, that would be enough. She would not have failed.

The funeral parlour had once been a school and services were conducted in its cavernous assembly hall, which had a vertiginous mezzanine with long staircases in the four corners that led to rooms leading off it. If you half-closed your eyes it looked like one of those Escher woodcuts they had all been so taken with when they were young, a series of impossible stairs in an impossible reality where things were not where they were supposed to be, and yet their very distortion, their out-of-placeness, was alluring, and for no reason at all this recalled to her a friend from her student days and she wondered what had happened to her since. It seemed such a long time ago.

Meanwhile, Neville was droning on: would he ever finish? And then, out of the fog of his words a bracing thought came to her, the first moment of clarity since Nick abandoned her: *I wonder if that church is still for sale.*

PART 2

the conversion

18

Her sister, Isobel, rings and announces she is coming for the weekend. She is in need of a break, and besides, she is curious. 'What have you got yourself into this time, Cookie?' she says, in that peremptory tone she has, the voice of a director of nursing in a large hospital, which she is.

Isobel is only three years older but for most of their lives it might as well have been ten, so superior is her attitude. The eldest child, and all that that entails, and the only person who still calls Zoe by her childhood name, which had come into being, according to family folklore, because her father had pronounced her good enough to eat.

Isobel arrives just after three on the Friday afternoon in her big Subaru wagon and gives her a warm hug. 'This is charming,' she says, 'up here on a rise like this, with all the vineyards.'

'We can do the cellar-door thing tomorrow if you like.'

'Good.' They enter the vestibule and Isobel pauses and looks around. 'Very bare,' she says. 'It could do with some flowers.' Only two minutes in and already giving advice.

'It's a threshold, and I need to think about that. What's the first thing I want to see when I open the door?'

'You sound like Nick. Overthinking it.'

Ah, already Nick is to be mentioned. No inhibition from Isobel. It's as if he died years before, when he was Isobel's boyfriend, not Zoe's. For Isobel and Nick had a brief fling when they were students, before Zoe even met him, and they enjoyed a kind of comradely intimacy ever after to a degree that Zoe could find irritating, as when Isobel condescendingly pronounced on his character and foibles as if she had more insight into them than Zoe, who was, in Isobel's words, blinded by hormones. Isobel prides herself on not being blinded by anything.

Once inside, Isobel drops her overnight bag on the floor and begins to peer at the plaques. 'Oh, this is a good one,' she pronounces.

IN MEMORIAM

Evelyn Rosina Curthoys

1897–1976

Of guileless lips and universal charity

'And who wouldn't want a wife like Rosina? Not the kind to get Adam munching on an apple.' She laughs and looks around. 'Where am I sleeping?'

'On the couch or in the double bed with me.'

'I'll take the bed.'

They eat early, Isobel exclaiming at the primitive nature of the kitchen: 'It's like camping inside,' she says, 'and you used to have such a big kitchen.'

'I used to have a lot of things.'

By six-thirty it has cooled a little and they move outside to sit on fold-up chairs and contemplate the vine-yards below.

'The graveyard,' Isobel says.

'Across the road.'

'I suppose it's full of old pioneers.'

'I've never looked. Haven't got around to it.'

Isobel fixes her with a mock glare. 'Typical.' And resting her empty glass on the dry yellow grass: 'Let's go. I feel like a walk. All that driving and my back has seized up.'

Zoe sighs. She has been resisting the graveyard and until now avoided it, but as usual Isobel dictates the agenda. 'Wear a pair of my boots,' she says. There are clumps of agapanthus there and according to the locals the snakes like to curl up in them.'

They stroll down the driveway in the golden light and cross the road to where an old wooden gate encrusted with lichen opens onto a jumble of headstones. The graves are mostly old and in varying states of decay, but this only makes them seem more picturesque: the warmth of the stone, the soft curlicues of the carving, the rusted iron surrounds with their fleur-de-lis tips. Over the years the geometry of the headstones has been softened by flower-ing weeds and bushes. Sprouted from seeds excreted by birds, they have grown tall and dense until they obscure the faded inscriptions on the headstones. It's all so unlike the rows of bare rectangles, the sterile neatness and the wilting flowers of the modern graveyard on the other side of the town.

Zoe does her best to ignore the headstones but Isobel is intent, always a demon for detail and reading aloud from them in a way that gets under Zoe's skin, as if they are tourists in Hades. *Shut up, Isobel*, she thinks, *just shut up*. A breeze comes up, and she feigns a chill and suggests they return to the church for a nightcap, but Isobel is bending over to peer at a very ordinary headstone framed by wild correa.

'Christ,' she murmurs, staring open-mouthed with an expression of horror. 'Look at this.' The year is 1919 and three sisters, aged five, nine and thirteen, had died within a week of one another. They were buried together, along with their mother, who had died exactly nine months later. Nine months: the time it took to gestate a child. 'Spanish flu,' says Isobel.

They retreat in silence to the church. By now it is almost dark and the lights that Zoe turned on before they left shine through the windows so that the little church glows like a beacon on the hill. She has not before come home to it lit up in the night and for the first time she is struck by its mellow beauty, as if it were a giant lantern resting on the earth.

Inside, she opens an expensive bottle of local vintage bought especially for Isobel and they sit on the couch, both feeling more subdued than when they ventured out.

'You can see why I avoid graveyards,' Zoe says.

'People were different then. They faced death more often. They were tougher. Like Nan.'

'Yes.'

'Sometimes I dream of her.'

'Really. Doing what?'

'Usually giving me advice.' Isobel raises her eyebrows as if to say: *What else?*

'Well, she *was* bossy.'

Together, in the candlelight, they return to their time as children with Una. Una the survivor. Orphaned at five, fostered by an abusive family, roused early every morning to clean school classrooms in her foster mother's business, beaten in a blanket if she stole food. Later in life she would do seasonal work picking hops in Myrtleford. In the autumn school holidays their father would drive them to stay with her, to sleep in coarse army cots beside her bed in one of the primitive hop-pickers' huts, built in a row near a creek lined with prickly blackberry bushes grown wild. At four they rose in the dark to ride on the flatbed tray of a lorry to the hop fields, legs dangling over the side, elated at the bone-jolting bounce from the bumps along the rutted track. And then the fields in the pre-dawn light, a paradise of delicate green vines laden with cones the colour of pale jade and shaped like tiny paper lanterns, the intoxication of the smell, the heady bitter resin, and later, damper with jam and billy tea over an open fire, the smoke stinging their eyes, and running through the vines with other children, shouting, until, exhausted, they bounced in Una's big hessian bin, which by then was full of hops. Later, the weighing of the day's pick and the ride home on the lorry at dusk, the smell of hops in their clothes and hair, home to the dark hut lit by a kerosene lamp where Una cooked supper over a woodfired stove.

For them it had been Eden, until one season a toddler from one of the huts nearby had been thrown into an open sewerage pit by two older children and drowned. And then it was no longer Eden, and there was no Eden.

Isobel is staring up at the figure of Jesus, a shepherd's crook in one hand, a child in the other. 'Those windows, Cookie, do they bother you?'

She lies. 'After a while you don't see them.'

'They'd bother me.' Isobel is looking tired. 'It's good to be here, Cookie. It's good to have all this space. I thought it might feel creepy…' She doesn't finish her sentence but looks up into the vault of the ceiling, then leans forward to loosen her thick chestnut hair so that it sits heavily on her shoulders. She is big-boned, like their father, and handsome. Somehow she looks at home in the nave; she is big enough for it, thinks Zoe.

'Funny you should end up working in a hospital.'

'Yes, isn't it.' This is an allusion to Zoe having abandoned her nursing training, something Isobel had disapproved of. She wants now to know about the little hospital at Crannock and Zoe finds herself taking an unexpected pride in being able to tell her that the hospital works surprisingly well (*I am not wasting my time here, Isobel*). The people in the town know they are lucky to have it. The state government had mooted closing it as a cost-cutting measure and only the representations of the local member for parliament in what is a marginal seat had saved it, for now, anyway. What they need is doctors. Adil Khalid works long hours while locums come and go. To soften the edge of her sister's forensic curiosity she relates some of the more amusing episodes in her work and succeeds in making Isobel laugh so that eventually, in a good mood, they are able to drink a little too much and feel the comfort of that unspoken understanding that only a blood tie can summon.

They sleep in the big bed, side by side, as they did when they were children. In the bed that Nick had once slept in, Nick with whom they had both slept, at different times and on other nights. Zoe had asked him once why he had married her and not Isobel. She wasn't feminine, he said. It was like fucking another man, like a short intense work-out in a gym. She was quick to arousal, quick to orgasm and afterwards had no interest in any languorous chitchat, just wanted to get up and get on with things. He did not feel a sense of her ultimate surrender, felt that she always kept something in reserve, a remark Zoe had thought nothing of at the time.

By then she had learned that for Nick there was always an underlying disappointment with sex, an acute case of post-coital sadness, as if once the gates of heaven had been breached the glowing field beyond proved to be a mirage. More than once he had lain beside her and reflected ruefully on the gap between the before and the after. How could an experience so all-consuming amount in the end to so little? After even the most annihilating rush the world remained the same. In a day, sometimes an hour, the effect wore off, the endorphins dissolved in the blood. No-one was saved.

Saved, Nick? Whoever expected to be saved? You wanted too much.

In the morning she drives Isobel to the Silver Wattle vineyard for brunch. Isobel has slept badly and woken from a troubling dream. A helicopter carrying a bleeding child had landed on the roof of the hospital. She had carried the child into the lift where the doors had stuck, and in a vortex of dread she had shouted and beaten on the doors but no-one could hear her, no-one had come. In the early morning, while Zoe slept, she had gone for a walk around the church grounds.

It's only a short drive to the vineyard but Isobel is uncharacteristically silent. They settle themselves at an outdoor table and Isobel tells of her dream. Like all troubling things it needs to be relived in order for its potency to be discharged, and Zoe listens with the degree of careful attention required of her, however incomprehensible the dream might prove to be to the listener, though in this case its meaning could not be more obvious. They ought not to have gone into the churchyard.

After they have eaten they linger in the sun and speak of their children, then return to the church for Isobel to gather her things together. When she has packed her overnight bag she strolls across to the altar to look at the books and sees beside them Nick's old chess set. 'My God,' she says, 'we used to have some battles over this.'

'I remember. It disappointed him that I wouldn't play.' As a child Zoe had hated chess, the iron logic of it. She and her mother preferred card games, with their flighty element of chance. Isobel, meanwhile, is fingering the queen. She says nothing, but Zoe knows what she is thinking: she had been fond of Nick and she misses him. Zoe had meant to tell her about the girl but somehow the right time had never arrived. And now it's too late. Not here, not in the church.

In the vestibule, as she is leaving, Isobel looks around and spots the wooden plaque: *O Lord deliver us from our present fallen life.* 'Where have we fallen *from*, Cookie?' she murmurs, and, not waiting for an answer: 'You need to decorate this space—it's too bare. Put your own stamp on it.'

Her *stamp*. It seems a preposterous idea, as if she could just sweep in and cancel the history of a building with a few knick-knacks. Within its stone walls she can do almost anything, but as she had intuited from the beginning, this would only be a disguise, a camouflage of something essential that would persist. She would still be living in a monument on a hill that had laid claim not just to the land around it but to a way of life, a moral universe that is hers and yet not hers. She has come there to exorcise a ghost and so far that hasn't worked. The ghost has merely taken licence to appear when it pleases.

19

At the farmers' market on a Sunday morning the stalls are set up under an avenue of plane trees that in autumn offer little shade. Wandering through the dense crowd with her hessian shopping bag and feeling comfortably rustic, before long Zoe finds herself gazing down at a trestle table laid with braids of purple garlic. Overhead is a striped awning and behind the table sits a woman close to her own age with flawless skin and ash-blonde hair. The carefully braided bulbs make her think of a statue in the National Gallery of a harvest goddess with a plait reaching to her waist, and while she is wondering if she could use that much of the pungent bulb over the coming months, a man enters through the back flap of the tent carrying two coffees and she recognises the Reverend Patrick Carter.

'Hello, I'm Zoe North,' she says. 'I bought St Martin's.'

'So I heard.' He hands one of the coffees to the blonde woman. 'How are you managing there?' And before she can reply: 'This is my wife, Peggy.' And she and Peggy nod and smile at one another, but there are buyers jostling at her elbow and a woman shouting in her ear: 'I say, is this the Ethiopian stuff?' Zoe is in the way of trade

but manages to blurt out: 'May I come and see you some-
time? I'd like to know about the history of the church.'

'Sure,' he says. 'We're in the book. Give us a ring.'

At the end of the street the roof of her car is littered
with leaves the colour of rust and turmeric that have
dropped from the plane tree directly above. How bright
they are, and yet how dry. In the small adjacent park she
recognises Dr Khalid's wife, who is pushing a child on one
of the swings. She knows little of the hospital staff; after
work they retreat to their small bush holdings or commute
to one of the bigger towns in the valley. She is not one
of them. When Lachie had asked if she were lonely, she
could answer truthfully that she was not; for now her situation suited her and she need not think beyond the coming
week. That was the point of her retreat. She has no plan
for the conversion and is no better than reactive, and even
then only when in a low mood. 'I am squatting,' she says
to herself as she opens the car door, and the empty vestibule tells the tale.

That night, for the first time since arriving at the church,
she dreams of Nick. There is a tapping at one of the
windows, faint at first, and then louder, almost enough to
wake her. He has positioned a ladder against the outside
wall on the eastern side and is knocking against the
window of the three apostles. She knows it's him because
she can see his face pressed against the glass and lit with
a sickly yellow glow from the cloak of one of the apostles.

He is agitated and saying something, and while his tone is urgent she can't make out the words. And then, 'It's my church,' he's shouting, 'let me in,' and beating with his fist against the fragile solder, so that she thinks the glass might shatter. And now he is in the bed beside her, propped against a stack of pillows with a pad on his knees, scribbling notes, and it's as if a live current of electricity is pulsing beneath the sheet. He is irritable. 'You haven't done anything to the place,' he says, 'you need me here to get on with it.' She takes his hand and rests it on her thigh, but he removes it and stabs his pen into the page.

She wakes. The light on her phone shows 5.22. She gets out of bed, unlocks the church door and steps outside into the early dawn in her flimsy nightgown, turning towards the window of the apostles and half-expecting to see an empty ladder.

The air is sweet and still, and she sits on the stone steps in front of the big door and waits for the birds, who must soon begin to stir. Nick's presence is palpable. He is beside her on the steps, he is strolling on the dry grass, he is under the macrocarpa pines inspecting the electric fence, he is on the roof peering into the empty belltower. He has taken possession, but not for long. Tonight she will have other dreams and the bittersweet nostalgia that enfolds her now will by tomorrow morning have faded into mere memory.

Inside, she dresses slowly. She is hesitant, as if each item of clothing is new to her and yet somehow superfluous.

She makes coffee and leaves it to grow cold. At the door of the church, belatedly, she remembers her keys.

She drives slowly towards the hospital because the surface of the road is not entirely real; it blurs at the edges and the white line at its centre is a thin, shimmering haze. The trees on either side are only half there, lovely but remote, and the car itself seems to hover above the bitumen until, out of nowhere, a dual-cab ute rears up behind her, blasting its horn before overtaking her. The dog in the tray at the back is untethered, windblown and cheerful, its tongue lolling in the breeze.

In the midafternoon Gail McVilly arrives at the hospital for a meeting of the board. She waves to Zoe as she strides through the reception area wrapped in a shawl of paisley silk.

Since her appointment Zoe has learned more about Gail: that she is a former public servant who, a decade ago, gave up a senior executive position in the state government and bought an olive farm in the valley. She is an imposing woman, tall and slender, with a halo of thick auburn hair and shoulders invariably draped with a long, flowing shawl. Her pale skin is freckled in an attractive way and she has a perfect set of ultra-white teeth. Though she is some years younger than Zoe, she addresses her in a friendly, forthright way as if she were the elder, but she speaks to everyone like that.

Later, on her way out, Gail comes to Zoe's office

and stands in the doorway. 'How are you finding it?' she asks. Zoe assumes she means the job but Gail waves her arm dismissively and says: 'No, no, the old church.' And without waiting for an answer: 'Come to dinner one night. I'll be in touch.'

On the Friday she finds a note on her desk, an invitation from Gail to dinner on Saturday week. *I like to eat early*, the note says, *so come at 5.30*. It's a summons.

20

She dresses carefully, for she has not been out in a long time and is surprised at how much she is looking forward to it. In recent days her curiosity about the little town has begun to grow and Gail, Zoe has been told by one of the nurses, 'knows everyone'.

The house is a long, low-slung bungalow of mud brick that years before had formed the hub of a short-lived commune. The name of the commune, 'Windsong', remains on a wooden sign at the entrance to a steep drive that winds through an olive plantation until it reaches the house, which sits just below the brow of the hill. To one side, in a solitary spot on a grassy flat, a startlingly white enamel bath stands on cast-iron legs, filled with marigolds of a brazen orange and yellow hue.

It's a warm, still evening—no wind song in the air— and they sit out on a concrete terrace painted in terracotta red. There are ten guests and Zoe knows none of them. Mango daiquiris are served on arrival and soon the long table is set with huge platters of shellfish on beds of ice, skillets of barbecued fish and octopus, along with immense wooden bowls of salad. Bottles of valley wine sit in silver ice buckets and along the centre of the table a line of waffle-patterned beeswax candles flicker and glow against the backdrop of undulating hills, rims of purple shadow.

The man on her left introduces himself as Ron. His wife she now recognises as Roseanne, a nurse at the hospital. Ron is talkative, in an engaging way. He is a coalminer and has worked at the Kerrigan colliery for twenty-four years. Now in his early sixties, he no longer goes underground but is part of a four-man clean-up team made up of older miners. 'Filthiest industry in the world.' He laughs. 'Me and my mate Vince joke that when we retire we'll join the greenies and campaign against it.' Then why does he stay in it? 'It's a good job. It's meant I can send my kids to the uni and they won't have to go down the mine.' He wants to know where she lives and she tells him about the church. 'Rosie and me were married there. Lovely spot. The churches always grab the best spots, don't they? I suppose the heritage lot have got their hands all over it. Pity. You could knock it down and use the stone to build something more comfortable.'

'If I knocked it down, what would I do with the stained-glass windows?'

'Reckon you could rearrange the bits into a different look. The hippies that built this place'—he nods at the house behind them—'used to make stained glass. Birds, butterflies, that kind of thing. Gail didn't like it. Had them taken out.'

'You mean I could recycle?'

'Yeah, that's the go now, isn't it?' And he winks at her.

Winking, she decides, is a thing in the valley.

Roseanne remarks on the sweetness of the fish—'red snapper, I reckon'—which prompts Ron to tell Zoe about the big cruiser he owns and his love of game fishing off the coast. 'Blue marlin,' he explains, 'world's biggest bony fish. One of the fastest swimmers there is.' He pulls out his phone. 'Here, look at this.'

Roseanne rolls her eyes. 'Zoe doesn't want to look at that.'

Ron ignores her. 'See, that's our boat.'

She looks at the video of the cruiser, three men in shorts at the stern, the boat pitching violently, the bright white of the craft against the brilliant blue of the ocean, something—a lure?—trailing at speed through the bubbling water and then a shout, and the great fish leaping up out of the surge, like an acrobat, twisting and writhing on the line, its blue-black back, its silver white underbelly, the long dorsal fin, the great staring eye, the gaping mouth and the thin spear that stabs the air high above the roiling foam beneath. 'This one's a psycho!' shouts one of the crew, and Ron laughs out loud, so that heads at the table turn to look in their direction. 'They fight hard,' he says.

'You don't eat 'em.' This from Roseanne. 'Too gamey. They toss 'em back.'

'Yeah, just good fun. It's a great feeling when you're in the fight chair.' *She looks like an animal-lover. Probably thinks I'm a right bastard. Who'd buy a church? Some city person with no clues about what it's going to cost them.*

Their plates are empty but for small piles of delicate pink prawn casings. The long table is in temporary disarray, salads gone limp in the heat, platters piled high with empty oyster shells and parts of octopus that have not found favour, thick segments of charcoalled tentacle with leathery suckers. These are cleared and dessert is served, a huge bombe of spun sugar that conceals layers of cake and ice-cream studded with glacé fruit. Gail produces a cellophane packet and spears the glistening top of the bombe with a handful of party sparklers that look like elongated needles of frozen ash. Their sparks fly up into the candlelight.

Ron and Roseanne get up to sit with friends at the other end of the table, and Ron nods amiably. 'We'll be seeing you around.' All the time that he has been speaking, the young man on Zoe's other side hasn't ventured a word. He is gazing now out over the valley and seems disinclined to talk, so she leans back in her chair and closes her eyes, content to soak in the warmth of the night. She has long passed the age when she feels uncomfortable with silence and finds herself suffused now with nostalgia, not for her former life but for something intangible, a quality lost and now found. It's not unpleasant, and may, she think, have something to do with the fineness of the valley wine.

But now Gail is at her shoulder. 'You've met my nephew?'

Zoe opens her eyes and a soft male voice says, obediently, 'Hello, I'm Simon.' Gail smiles benignly and pats his shoulder. 'Simon came down to attend a Buddhist retreat and I've bullied him into spending a night with his aunt before he goes back.' She speaks as if there is some silent joke between them, between her and all of them. A boisterous guest at the other end of the table shouts her name, beckoning her over, and she laughs and moves on with the loose and slightly inebriated swagger of the powerful hostess.

'It's okay,' Zoe says to Simon, 'we don't have to talk.'

But talk they do, and later she will find it interesting that she can recall more of her conversation with Ron than with Simon. She will remember Simon saying that during his retreat he had learned to live with silence and now he was finding it hard to speak at all, but he expected that when he got home he would, as he put it, 'relapse'. And then he says something about 'learning not to fear the void'. Or does he say that he had looked into the void and learned not to fear it?

These are the kinds of words that are difficult to recall with accuracy, whereas a man in a cruiser with a marlin on the end of his line is a more vivid image, or maybe it says something about her, Zoe thinks, that the one is more vivid than the other: the great fish with its long spike convulsing in the air. What image could anyone have of the void? How complacent I am now, she thinks. Is it detachment, or indifference? And for the first time the thought occurs to her that she need not do anything to the interior of the church, she need only to continue to camp there, in a kind of continuous present. *There is no need to do anything. Nothing at all. This is how people get by: a marlin on the end of the line, a Buddhist retreat, candles flickering in the dusk.*

The candles have burned low, blobs of yellow wax congealing around the rims of the candlesticks. And now at the other end of the table voices are raised. 'Poor bastards! The army chews them up and spits them out.' She hears the name Brayden Madden, and it's soon clear that they are discussing the young man's suicide. The man who had beckoned Gail over, Laurie, a member of the local council, is gesticulating at a glamorous middle-aged blonde opposite him. 'Some of them are mongrels,' she's saying. 'They shoot civilians.'

Laurie leans across the table and shakes his head. 'I wouldn't be casting any aspersions on Brayden Madden.'

'I didn't know Brayden Madden.' The blonde is curt. 'But I do know about the captain they're looking into who turns out, it seems, to have broken the rules of war.'

'The rules of war! Good God, woman, you go into a war to win, you do what it takes. That's been the problem with the bloody war. They've arsed around with half-measures.'

Ron, now seated at the other end of the table, is shaking his head. 'I think it's a bit unfair,' he says. 'We build them up as heroes and then we cut them down.'

The blonde holds her ground. 'That doesn't alter the fact of war crimes being committed. It's a national disgrace.'

To Zoe's surprise, Simon pipes up. 'Our troops have always been known for their brutality,' he says. 'When they were on leave during the First World War they used to throw Egyptians off trains for the fun of it.'

There is an uncomfortable silence.

Simon lowers his gaze to stare down at the tablecloth, glum, and instinctively Zoe knows what he is thinking. He has spent all those days in silence, and for what? Here he is, already reverting to the person he was before. What will it take?

Gail intervenes. 'What do you expect? We've all seen the documentaries, how they train those special forces. They brutalise them, then they send them off to a war where they're out in remote villages. They don't know who is the enemy and who isn't, and after too many tours of duty they're cynical and hardened, and we at home throw up our hands because they don't behave like officers and gentlemen.'

A candle flickers out. Gail stands and leans across to light it, and there is something in the deliberate gesture with which she blows out the match that closes the debate. A corner of her embroidered shawl has come loose and, tossing it back over her right shoulder, she surveys the table and takes command of the situation. 'It's time,' she says, 'we had some cheese.'

The outdoor lights have been turned on and moths flutter around the glowing spotlights fixed under the eaves. Simon bids Zoe a polite goodnight and moves away to say goodnight to his aunt. She watches as he kisses Gail on the cheek and then, as she grasps his hand and pulls him towards her, he embraces her stiffly and pulls back, and nodding to the rest of the table walks off and into the dark house.

Across the vacant space of Simon's empty chair a young woman is staring at Zoe. She is wearing a bright red shirt with a pattern of frogs on it, and she leans across now and extends her hand. 'Hello, I'm Melanie Doyle.'

Zoe thinks it an unexpected gesture in a young woman; there is something forthright and masculine about it. Her hand is warm and strong, the fingers blunt and square at the ends. The young woman has a broad face, close-cropped reddish-chestnut hair, a short neck and fine features that seem not quite to go with her sturdy body. They speak only briefly because Zoe is tired and all too aware that she has drunk too much, but she learns that Melanie teaches at the Crannock Secondary College and has been in the valley just over a year.

'I teach Drama,' she says, 'among other things,' in a way that implies the other things are of no importance. Zoe wonders at how she knows Gail and she says that Gail went to school with her mother. 'I hear you've bought a church,' she says. And then, to Zoe's surprise, 'May I come and visit you?'

'Are you interested in churches?'

'Not exactly.'

Zoe does not answer but instead rises from her chair and says that it's time for her to go. The effort of further conversation is beyond her. At the other end of the table she says goodnight to Gail and then, aware of a slight unsteadiness as if walking on soft sand, she ambles over to her car, which mercifully is no more than twenty metres away.

The long driveway down to the highway flies by in an olive-leaf blur and she sails out onto the bitumen in a kind of unheeding glide. The world has narrowed in, has lost its hard edges, is an amorphous body of night lit by the flare of headlights and a white line that curls around blind corners and not another car in sight, until she hears the wail of the police siren and a urgent rooftop light is flashing at her rear and she pulls over to the side of a road lined with shadowy bush. The uniformed man who appears at her window is middle-aged and looks vaguely familiar.

'Mrs North, isn't it?'

'Yes.' How does he know her name? Peering at him in the half-light, she recognises him. He is one of the officers who had been called to the reception area of the hospital just a week ago during a fracas between an estranged married couple. And after he had removed the husband, he had returned in the late afternoon to get a statement from Zoe and had looked so tired and drawn that she offered him a cup of tea, and they had sat drinking tea in the staff tearoom. Constable Cornes.

'You live in the old church.'

'Yes.' He looks around him. 'Wait here a minute, please.' And he walks back to the patrol car, where he bends into the window on the passenger side to confer with the other constable. Then he returns.

'If you'd like to move into the passenger seat, Mrs North, I'll drive you home.'

With the police car following they drive in silence. He does not attempt to make conversation and she is glad. Will he or will he not produce the breathalyser? Surely the moment has passed, and with a deep sigh she exhales and settles into the passenger seat, her eyes fixed on the road ahead, the shadowy paddocks on either side and the reliable monotony of the white line ahead.

It seems scarcely minutes before they are parked outside the door of the church. Without a word Cornes gets out of the car and before she can gather her wits he has opened the passenger door. 'Thank you,' she says, and climbs out, slowly and with the exaggerated composure of a woman who is inebriated. Once on her feet she leans back against the bonnet and he hands her the keys.

'More care next time, eh?'

'Thank you, officer.'

She manages to open the door without faltering. The patrol car has pulled up behind them, and Cornes stands in front of it and waits until she is inside the vestibule where she turns at the open door and waves, squinting at his stolid outline in the glare of the headlights and hoping to appear dignified rather than abject.

She has scarcely been inside a few minutes when the first of the stomach cramps grip her and she rushes to the lavatory to throw up. The cramps come in strong, surging waves and it's like childbirth, she thinks, not quite as annihilating but not far off it, the slow, aching contraction and then the heaving and the acid burn in the throat. In between each spasm she sits slumped on the floor, her legs splayed, her back resting against the cool, hard stone of the font, until at last the waves began to weaken, to flatten and grow further apart. Hoisting herself to her feet, she steadies against the rim of the font. Bent over from exhaustion and clutching her abdomen, she trips against the coarse fringe of the Turkish rug, falling to her knees with a groan and crawling like an animal to her bed.

On her back, dazed and still nauseated, she gazes up at the shadowy image of St Martin, a slurry of deranged colour. She is cold now, very cold, and she draws the light cotton cover up to her chin, grateful for how the pain of the body can offer relief from the turbulence of the mind. In the morning the hangover, she thinks, will be worth it, and, as she drifts into sleep, the image of the great marlin soars in her mind's eye, writhing on the line, spearing the air and fighting for its life with no intimation that it is soon to be released.

21

On the Monday morning Mick Hanlon rings her at work. He is ready to remove the font. A date had been set before and changed twice but now it is all good, he has disposed of a few other commitments, and he can do it on the coming Saturday.

Just after nine on the agreed day Mick turns up with his son, Travis, Mick driving the Genie lift, which lumbers up the drive at a crawling pace like a giant praying mantis while Travis slouches behind with the distracted air of a boy who would rather be somewhere else. She fears the lift will not fit through the entrance door but Mick has measured it up and is confident that, with the neck of the crane collapsed, as on a fire truck, there won't be a problem. She offers him and Travis coffee and cake before they start but Mick declines. 'We'll just get on with it. Might take a while.'

The first step is to sever the font and its stem from its stone base, using fine hacksaw blades to cut through the joint holding them together. 'Lucky,' pronounces Mick, 'no iron pins holding them together. Last thing you want.' Then they hook a square metal frame onto the lift and lever the font onto it before securing it with what looks like leather straps but turns out to be some kind of fabric. At which point Travis begins the process of winding the handles on the lift to raise the font so it can be lifted away from the base—'Easy there, Trav, take it slow'—and transported out through the vestibule and onto the back of the utility that Mick has driven in. All the while Zoe holds her breath, fearing a debacle, a judgment of the gods. But all goes smoothly.

The next step is to lift the stone base off the floor, the drainage pipe embedded in it like a rigid snake. Following the same process, it is soon outside on the tray of the ute and she is staring down through a hole in the floorboards at the dusty brick foundations beneath. They will come back another day and patch the floor, Mick says, nothing to worry about, she won't be getting possums up through there that night, and they will have that cup of coffee now if that's all right. He lays a sheet of old plywood over the gap and there is much less dust than she had anticipated.

'You'll be wanting to do something about that.' Mick nods in the direction of the lavatory and shower.

She sighs. 'Yes.'

'Know a good plumber.'

'I think I need more than a plumber.'

'Reckon you do.' He grins. 'Know a good builder.'

'Still thinking about it, Mick.' Dropping the personal pronoun was catching.

'Don't bloody wonder. Big job. Woman on her own.

Anyway,' he looked around as if making a professional assessment, 'you look comfortable enough.'

'I am.' He is well disposed towards her, not least because she has paid him in cash, tipped Travis and is giving Mick the font when she might have sold it. Apart from anything else, his mother had been a stalwart of the congregation.

All the while, Travis has barely uttered a word. She thinks he could not be more than eighteen, a stringy youth with lank black hair to his shoulders, finely built, unlike his father, and shy. He hasn't once looked her in the eye and seems an odd offspring to have been produced by two confident adults.

That night she sits contemplating the empty space in the floor and feels as if an amputation has been carried out. She recalls her conversation with Neville Glass when he had expounded on Alexander's theory of the unity of centres, each with its own intense life that contributes to the coherence of the whole. She had understood it only as a series of abstractions, but now, with the removal of the font, she sees that the unity of the whole has been tilted out of balance. The church had been a body, and now it has lost a limb. The buyer of a church must impose their own dream, which means they can only live in it if all trace of its original purpose is camouflaged or destroyed: 'As much as possible, vertical space (heaven) must be rendered horizontal (earth).' Somewhere she had read this, somewhere in Nick's notes, not that she still has them. After she had discovered his letter to Sophie she had burnt the lot, had lit a fire in a steel bucket at the side of the church and watched the smoke curl up towards the windows. Fragments of charred paper had fluttered in the flames and drifted off towards the sheep paddock where they had caught on the electrified fence.

All the next morning she veers between feeling unburdened—a new space, a new possibility—and bereft. In the afternoon she drives to a nearby nursery and buys an enormous terracotta pot planted with a tall Kentia palm and directs the delivery man to stand it where the font had been. It would do for now. When Neville rings she will tell him that the site for redemption from original sin has been replaced by *Home Beautiful*. And that he was right. A church cannot be made other, cannot be undivided. She sees now that as soon as possible everything must go, and that includes the windows. The removal of the font has given her clarity. At the end of the month she will get a quote from a glazier. She will dip into what remains of her capital and make arrangements to strip the place.

She had read in the local newspaper that the museum in the mining town of Menandah, thirty kilometres to the north of Crannock, had won an award for small museums in the regional category. There was a photograph of the curator, Michael Draper, and now she rings the museum and asks to speak to him. Would he be interested in some stained-glass windows? 'They're exceptional quality,' she says.

'I don't think so,' says the cool voice at the other end of the phone, 'but I'd like to see your church.' They agree on five-thirty for an after-work drink.

Draper does not come alone but brings with him a young woman. Simone is his assistant and drives him around. 'I have a car phobia,' he says, with an air of brisk confidence that belies this statement.

'Must be difficult for you living in the country.'

'There are always friends. And trains.'

Simone looks to be fresh out of art school, with short black hair in fine layers, artfully bleached so that the tips are yellow. She wears big round glasses with bright pink rims, striped tights and workman's boots.

Zoe pours them each a glass of wine, and with glasses in hand they begin a tour of the windows. 'So these wouldn't interest you?'

'Not really. They're actually pretty good specimens. Better than many others I've seen. Perhaps if there was one that memorialised a local person. Or something generic but relevant, like a miner. That could be of interest.' He pauses in front of the window of St Martin. 'They really are rather fine. The artist had a lightness of touch.'

She tells him about the Salome windows and he grimaces. 'Not something you'd want to contemplate before your Sunday roast,' he says.

Simone, meanwhile, is gazing up at the big triptych above the altar. 'The usual jocks,' she says breezily. 'They look airbrushed.'

'How do you mean?'

'All perfectly formed. Neat hair, trim beards. No Semitic noses.' She giggles. 'Clothes a fisherman wouldn't have been able to afford.'

Michael looks at her and smiles indulgently. 'You're in a church, Sim.'

'Well, they're not very ethnic, are they?'

'I think they're meant to represent an ideal.' Zoe is terse.

'Mmm…' murmurs Draper ruminatively. Recognising the need for tact, he retreats from Simone's callow mockery and strolls over to the altar steps, where he gazes up at the big triptych above the reredos: the scarlet and gold cloaks, the ageless heads with radiant halos. 'The iconography is unexceptional,' he says, 'but lovely colouration, some of the best work I've seen. That crimson glass costs a fortune. But look, even if we wanted them, getting them out would be a nightmare. By now they'd be brittle. They're quite stable when they're standing vertically but when you take them out and lay them down they go all floppy. They can be re-soldered but that would be costly, and they don't have enough historical significance to warrant a hole in my budget.'

She asks if he knows of the Holman Hunt–inspired window in the abandoned St Stephen's and he says no, he doesn't, but he will go and have a look. That could interest him more. Has a bit of a story behind it, though not a local one.

Simone meanwhile is peering at the plaques along the walls and is almost back at the entrance when she calls out. 'Look at this, Michael.' Though she is some distance from where he is standing beside Zoe at the altar steps, Simone barely has had to raise her voice.

Draper turns towards her, and then back to Zoe. 'The acoustics here are good.'

'So everyone says.'

She offers them another drink and to her surprise they accept. They settle in the sitting area and she asks how long they have been in the district. Simone has come from Sydney to work for a year as an intern, but Draper and his wife have lived in Crannock for two years. His wife is a teacher at the local secondary college. Zoe confesses that she hasn't yet been to the museum, and he describes it as being mostly focused on the history of agriculture and mining but he plans to broaden it out from there if he can find patrons. Money, he says, is tight, and it occurs to her then that he might have seen her as a potential donor. He plans soon to curate an exhibition of the local Indigenous nations, he says. Does he know Berenice Hanlon, she asks. No, he doesn't. I'll give you her contact details, she says, wondering if he will be prepared to incorporate Berenice's account of the McAlister massacre.

It's almost seven when they leave. They shake hands at the door and he invites her to visit the museum. He will take her around it himself.

22

The Reverend Patrick Carter lives in a northern corner of
the valley, a forty-minute drive from the centre of town.
His garlic fields lie on the flat: long green rows of densely
planted bulbs with leafy stalks low to the ground. His
house sits on a rise, a concrete box with floor-to-ceiling glass
walls, so different from the church and its lancet windows
with their pointed arch. The ultra-modern window is as
big as it can be, while the church windows are formally
contained, and it strikes her for the first time that one of
the most distinctive things about a church is the experience it offers of space within enclosure, the opposite of the
modernist house that is all about the view and gazing out
to the horizon, something she and Nick had both disliked.
'Like living in a goldfish bowl,' Nick had said.

She remarks on this to Carter.

'Well, yes,' he says, with a smile that she finds condescending, 'the idea of the church began when nature was
regarded as harsh, as it was in European winters, and the
church offered protection. In Asian countries with hot
climates you'll notice that temples are very often open to
the air.'

And the stained glass?

'The windows were a form of teaching for the illiterate members of the congregation.'

She tells him of her recent visit to St John the Baptist's and her surprise at the Salome window.

He gives a vicar's polite chuckle. 'Well, the Old Testament is savage in parts.'

They sit in a light, airy living room where the first thing that compels her attention is an enormous wool tapestry on the far wall. It must be three metres by two, a bold composition of red waratahs and white proteas with an almost hectic quality, as if a flower might burst from the frame and the wool unravel in the air. Carter notes her stare and says: 'My wife, Peggy, is a weaver.'

She has never before seen a white protea and is struck by how their white outer petals are black at the tips and look as if they are the feathers of small birds plucked and arranged to simulate a flower. They give the tapestry an uncanny quality, not altogether appealing. 'It's wonderful,' she says. 'Are there waratahs in your garden?'

'We've planted two trees here but it's early days. They grow best after a fire.'

There is no sign in the room of religious iconography and she wonders if, somewhere in another room, they keep a private altar. She wants to ask why he decided to cultivate garlic but the question seems oddly personal, as if it might conceal an unspoken reproach: *Why aren't you doing good works? Isn't that your trade?* Instead, she returns to the subject of the windows. 'I've come to appreciate that the windows in St Martin's are very fine, and I wondered if you knew who made them.'

'No idea. The records don't tell us.'

'They must have been very expensive at the time. And Crannock is a small town.'

'Yes, but these country churches were mostly built on the profits of wool and some of the early beneficients were no doubt very devout.'

Beneficient. A priest's word. She asks if he misses not having a church.

'The Pentecostals would say that God is everywhere. You can conduct a service in your living room if that's what you're comfortable with.'

Would he do that?

'If I were asked to, yes.'

So he is not a traditionalist?

'In some things.'

He wouldn't have considered moving the altar into the centre of the church?

'Not at St Martin's. The nave is too narrow. We'd have been tripping over ourselves.' He smiles. 'There are liturgical reformers who would like to centre things more in the congregation, like theatre-in-the-round, so to speak, but you have to be practical. Sometimes there just isn't the space.'

She frowns and shifts in her seat. How thin and brittle is their conversation, and yet how could it be otherwise?

They have no connection and she comes with no entitlement. If they are dancing on straw, the fault is hers. She is an imposter; she hasn't come to learn about the history of the church at all; now that she is sitting with him, face to face, she recognises that she has come to seek his counsel on the violence of love, but instead they are talking about moving furniture around.

Your credo, she wants to say, what power has it over obsession? What remedy for the pain endured, for the damage inflicted? Nothing in your gospels has anything useful to say about the overpowering urge to possess another's body, or be possessed, to experience for a time the dissolution of the burden of self even at the risk of annihilation. And what is the meaning of this cruel and yet somehow natural havoc? Why is it that the road to heaven is the same path as the road to hell? Why is it that our deepest desires and our strongest drives are irreconcilable?

But no. Caught in the silky web of his professional courtesy, in the stillness and picturesque charm of his living room, she can find no way in, and there are only the picture windows, and the waratahs and the proteas. Better the bleeding man on the cross.

'I'm troubled by the altar,' she says (still on the furniture). She wonders if he could suggest what she might do with it.

'Well, it's something you might put in a garden. Or you could try asking one of the other churches in the valley if they have any use for what you want to dispose of.'

'It's been suggested to me that I break up the stone of the altar and turn it into a wall.' This had been Lachie's idea, but to repeat it is a provocation. She has begun, unreasonably, to resent Carter's reserve, and this is peevish. He owes her nothing.

'I should think that might be a very useful thing to do. Stone walls can be very lovely.'

Clearly the man is a diplomat, and the more they talk the more she feels nosy and presumptuous, gauche even, but also aggrieved. In the end their conversation becomes an account of the list of repairs he had overseen, the size of the parish ('shrinking') and the failure of the bishop to turn up for the deconsecration. 'A misunderstanding. But we had a very nice picnic outdoors.'

'I see.' And she smiles back at him in a sour way that she hopes makes it clear that she knows she has been subjected to a calculated blandness. 'And the wall plaques?'

He suggests the obvious: offer them to the local museum and history room.

She tells him then of McAlister's visit and it's the only time she observes a tremor in his composure, though only slight, and he does not comment. Having dealt with her to his satisfaction, he changes the subject. How is she getting on at the hospital? Dr Khalid is a fine man and they are lucky to have him. And then Peggy appears, and with the practised discretion of a clerical wife dealing with parishioners reminds him of an appointment.

But there is one more thing she wants to say, in fairness to the man, and that's how affecting she had found his speech at Brayden Madden's funeral. 'I couldn't help noticing that you didn't mention God,' she says, and immediately regrets her rudeness.

'No need. God was there in the hearts of those present.'

'Those who believed.'

'Whether they believed or not.'

The man is opaque, like a window with no figuration, just a large panel of milky glass. And yet, for the first time since arriving, she softens towards him. Yes, whether they believed or not, something had been there that bound them together, and Carter had the grace to summon it.

He rises and escorts her to the front door, where he stands on the paved steps and surveys the fields below with satisfaction. He offers her a cheery wave. 'A conversion is a very difficult enterprise,' he says. 'Best of luck with yours.'

23

It's a Saturday afternoon at the hospital and a young woman enters through the automatic doors and looks around. 'Do you have an appointment?' Zoe asks. 'No,' she says, 'but I need to see a doctor.'

It's Melanie Doyle. At first Zoe doesn't recognise her from their brief meeting at Gail McVilly's dinner party, for she looks terrible. Her hair stands up in tufts, her eyes are red, her face puffy, her voice thick. She collapses onto one of the brown vinyl couches in reception with her legs splayed, blows her nose loudly and stares dolefully up at the television set perched high on a ledge where no-one can interfere with it, even though the sound can barely be heard.

'Dr Khalid is booked up today,' Zoe says, 'and I'm afraid we still haven't found a locum.' It's already four, but as fate would have it the phone rings and there is a late cancellation.

After Melanie has seen Dr Khalid, she emerges looking a little brighter. She pauses by the reception counter. 'My asthma,' she says, unbidden. 'I stupidly let my puffer run out and then I got a cold and it got worse.'

There is nothing for her to sign but she lingers. 'May I come and visit you?' she asks. 'I'd love to see your church.' There is in her manner an almost childlike forwardness. Unwell as she is, she exudes a brazen energy.

'Are you interested in churches?'

'Yes.'

'Really?' Zoe finds her response unconvincing and can't imagine why she would want to visit. 'Well, drop by some time.' She is deliberately vague.

'What about next Saturday afternoon?'

She could lie and say she won't be there but for some reason she doesn't. 'All right, come around three.'

And she does, to the minute, cruising up the drive in of all things a white Colorado ute, the tray of which, as far as Zoe can make out, is filled with old doors. When she remarks on the ute Melanie says yes, she needs it for moving stuff around.

'And you're feeling better?'

'Much better, thanks.' She gives an almost girlish smile, like a child on an outing, but then her demeanour changes and she stands with her hands on her hips and stares up at the roof of the church. 'Nice roof,' she says, 'in good nick,' as if she is a tradesman appraising a job. There is nothing girlish about Melanie, Zoe decides. Inside, she accepts the offer of a drink and begins immediately to wander around the church. 'Great,' she says, 'it's so intact. That's great.'

'Is it?'

Ignoring Zoe's question, Melanie climbs the stairs to the pulpit. Looking up into the rafters she declaims: 'To the gods a year is as a minute.' She pauses. And then: 'If you would storm heaven, storm it with your prayers.' And stands with her eyes closed. 'The acoustics are wonderful,' she says. 'Michael said they were.'

'Michael?'

'Michael Draper.'

'You know him?'

'I teach at the school with his wife, Stephanie.' At the bottom of the stairs she takes a deep breath. 'I've come to ask a favour.'

'Really.'

'The school puts on a performance every year.'

And now Zoe knows what is coming.

'All we have is the school gym, which is soulless and has crap acoustics. So I'm looking for another venue.'

'You do realise this is my home.'

'Yes, but Michael said you hadn't yet begun to renovate it and that the old fittings were still intact.' She looks around. 'They'd make marvellous props.'

'Props?' Zoe can only stare at her, bemused.

'Yes. The altar, those steps, the pulpit, the wide ledges on the windows—some of the actors could sit on those...' She stops. 'Was there a baptismal font here?'

'I had it removed.'

'Could you get it back?'

Her presumption is breathtaking. 'Why would I do that?'

Melanie doesn't answer but purses her lips as if weighing up the odds. 'I hope you don't mind me saying so, but you haven't got much furniture. It would be easy to move it to the side and bring in some chairs for the audience.'

Seeing Zoe speechless, she presses on. 'They're mounting arts events in the cathedral in the city now, did you know? Music concerts, short plays, poetry recitals. The cathedral charges a fee. Helps with the upkeep, and cheaper for performers than a theatre.'

'Yes, but the bishop doesn't live in the cathedral. And my pews are very uncomfortable.'

Irony is lost on her. 'People could bring a cushion. And we would bring in some chairs. You wouldn't have to lift a finger.'

'You do realise you'd have no toilet facilities.'

'Portaloos. We'd hire a couple.'

'I thought you had a limited school budget.'

'I'll pay for them myself if I have to.' She could not be more direct. And despite her bluntness, her frank opportunism, Zoe cannot help but admire the fact that she hasn't gushed, hasn't attempted to flatter or charm her.

'I don't think so, Melanie,' she says. 'This is not a public space, it's my home.' But now she finds herself choking on that word *home*. How odd that word sounds, not quite true, not quite false. Like everything in this space: provisional. One big *maybe*.

She offers Melanie another drink but the young woman declines. She has a rehearsal at five, she says. Zoe walks her to the ute and, on the way, asks her what she is staging for the school.

'It's a play by the Swedish playwright Strindberg. You probably haven't heard of him. No-one here has.'

She's right, Zoe hasn't. Nick and she were not what Neville referred to as theatre people. 'What's your play about?'

'It's called *A Dream Play*. It's almost never staged because it's too...' Melanie's voice trails away. 'It's considered too difficult. The school used to do stuff like *Grease* and *Mamma Mia!* but I've got a good bunch of kids this year and they deserve something better. The principal gives me a hard time but it's my call and that's the kind of mindset this town suffers from. These kids are seventeen and eighteen. They can do anything they put their minds to.'

She opens the door of the ute. 'Perhaps you'd like to come to a rehearsal and have a look. Tuesdays, Wednesdays and Thursdays at four in the school gym.'

'Not really my thing, Melanie.'

'Well, think about it'—as if this were some kind of generous offer. And she releases the handbrake and roars off down the hill, the old doors clattering in the back of the ute.

When Zoe returns to the church she pauses beneath

the pointed arch that separates the vestibule from the nave. How odd, she thinks, that the church feels emptier than it had before Melanie Doyle arrived. There is in her robust presence a certain quality, something resolute and enlivening. Though she is plain in looks (short, untidy, stocky), she is large in her being, more so than when Zoe encountered her at Gail McVilly's, where she would have said she was nondescript. It was odd how, once inside the church, she had seemed at home in it, like an actor who, on mounting a stage, feels that she is at last in her natural— her rightful—space.

Melanie is not one to waste time. On the following Saturday, a second visit and Melanie at the church door in white overalls splashed with pink and orange paint.

'Hi, Zoe. Just thought I'd drop by. Any second thoughts?'

She might have laughed out loud. 'Not a one.'

'I wish you'd come to a rehearsal.' And when Zoe does not respond, but simply purses her lips, Melanie produces a document from the deep pocket of her overalls. 'Here. Here's a script. It's a bit hard to follow in parts, so I've written out a precis for you.'

'If it's hard to follow, why would I want to read it, Melanie?'

'Because it might interest you.'

'You hope.' How odd it is that they speak to one another familiarly, almost teasingly, like a pair of schoolgirls.

'I'll leave it with you.' And she backs away towards the ute, which Zoe sees now is crammed with pieces of wood, old skirting boards, a pine fireplace surround, and three large garbage bags filled with God knows what.

'Are you renovating, Melanie?' she asks.

'No, I'm on the lookout for materials, for sets and props. This is a government school. No money to spare. I find stuff where I can and store it at Michael and Stephanie's place. They've got an old barn.' She climbs into the ute, toots the horn and reverses into the drive.

Zoe waits on the steps of the church. Will Melanie stop to shut the gates at the bottom? Sure enough, she simply blazes through the opening and swings out onto the road.

After she has walked down the drive to close the gates she returns to the nave and takes the script from the dining table, carries it to the altar, sits it on top of a pile of books and leaves it there.

That night she dreams of a grand cathedral, ornate and sombre. Cologne, again. The dark façade, the spiky towers, the great ship moored beside the train station. And the children are with her as before, Isaac and Tess. 'Look,' she says, 'here we are on the train again.' And the children stand at the window and gaze out with a dreamy expression, and all is well until the glass door of their compartment slides back and the train guard fills the doorway, and it's Melanie Doyle in a uniform of navy serge and a foreign-looking cap. Zoe is indignant. 'What are you doing in my dream?' she asks. 'I hardly know you.'

But Melanie doesn't respond. 'Where are your tickets?' she demands. Her voice is gruff, and Zoe rummages in her bag to find them. But her bag is empty. How can this be when just a few minutes ago it had been crammed with snacks for the children?

Panic seizes her. They will have to get off the train in a foreign country and look for Nick, who is nearby, though she can't be sure where. Nick will have the tickets. But why isn't he on the train? Where has he gone and why has he left them? Melanie is standing in the doorway in her strange uniform, waiting.

'I'm afraid,' Zoe begins, 'the tickets have gone missing—'

She wakes in a hot flush of dread.

24

In the college gym Zoe sits on a cracked chair of moulded plastic and waits for Melanie Doyle to register her entry. But Melanie is absorbed in the rehearsal.

It's true: the gym is grim, though no more so than any other of its kind. There are basketball markings on the shiny floor and hoops at either end. There are vinyl and wood vaulting-horses pushed against the walls and climbing ropes anchored to hooks and metal rings. Shabby tumbling mats of foam covered in grey cotton are stacked in a pile at one end. On the walls, high up, are honour boards with the names of sporting teams and individual athletes engraved in gold.

A group of senior students (she counts twelve) are seated in a wide circle at the centre of the court with what look like scripts on their knees. While Melanie paces around the perimeter, they take it in turns to read aloud, a kind of echoing gibberish that makes no sense. Melanie paces and paces, and sometimes she slaps the wooden pole that supports a hoop with the back of her hand, as if she is moving to an inaudible rhythm only she can detect in the muffled words that echo into the dusty air above the circle of chairs. She is relentless and, in her way, mesmerising. Then she stops, looks across, sees Zoe, and immediately beckons her over in a gesture both commanding and eager.

Zoe stands and walks to the edge of the circle. 'This is Mrs Zoe North,' Melanie says. 'She bought the old church outside town.' The cast, in school uniform of navy shirts and grey skirts and trousers, look up with blank faces and offer an indifferent nod or a 'Hi'.

And to her surprise she sees that Travis Hanlon is among them. He has a knitted beanie pulled down over his forehead, but she recognises the high cheekbones and the long black hair. Travis Hanlon: an unlikely participant, she would have thought, and perhaps the group's stage manager or set builder. She smiles at him, and he gives an awkward nod and lowers his eyes, and she regrets coming.

She opens her mouth to make her excuses when Melanie says, cheerily: 'We've blocked out the first twenty pages and we're about to have our first movement rehearsal. Please stay—you'll be surprised.'

Now it would be rude to leave and she retreats to her chair.

'Okay, guys!' Melanie claps her hands and with an assumed languor the troupe push back their chairs and slouch into positions beneath one of the hoops. Already they appear to know their lines, but so bad is the echo in the gym that Zoe has difficulty making out much of the dialogue, and in any case it seems incomprehensible.

After a respectable twenty minutes she catches Melanie's eye and points to her watch, whereupon Melanie strides over to her and says, bluntly, 'May I bring the cast to visit the church?'

Caught off guard, she is equally blunt. 'What on earth for?'

'Just to show them what good acoustics sound like. They have no idea how it can transform the words. You heard what it's like here. It would help them, I know it would. They're having trouble finding their groove.'

They're having trouble, she thinks, because you've chosen something unsuitable, something utterly beyond them. But Melanie's green eyes plead with her.

'When?'

'Whenever suits you.'

'It would have to be a weekend.'

'I'll find out when they can all come. Some of them have weekend jobs.'

She expects a call from Melanie, perhaps in a week or two, but no, three days later Melanie turns up on her way home from rehearsal.

'You're stalking me, Melanie.'

'You wouldn't be the first.'

'I haven't read the script, if that's what you're wondering.'

'I didn't think you would have, not yet. Just thought I'd drop by.'

She could ask why but she knows. Once this young woman has made up her mind that she wants something she is relentless. And there is something else: Zoe likes her. Perhaps, even, they like one another. Some kind of mutual recognition has taken place, but of what? *Re-cognise*: to know again something you had forgotten. 'Well, you might as well come in and have a drink.'

Melanie follows her to the little kitchen while she retrieves an open bottle from the fridge. 'This is like my kitchen,' Melanie says, 'as basic as it gets.'

'Basic is what I am.'

'Really? I wouldn't have said so.'

She ignores this and they settle at opposite ends of the couch. 'I was wondering, Mel…' She hesitates. 'Do people call you Mel?'

'Never. Don't like it. Don't do it.'

'I was wondering, Melanie, did you go to drama school?'

'Yeah, for a year. There were bimbos there with no brains who were better actors than I was. I could see I wouldn't get any work so I went and did a teaching degree.' She grins. 'Directing's more my speed. You get to choose the good stuff. You're not at other people's mercy. Who'd be an actor? Actors are puppets.'

'I suppose they are.'

Melanie has barely touched her wine but she holds her glass up now to the light, as if examining it for dross, and takes a long, considered swallow. And then: 'About that font. Can we get it back, even if only for a loan?'

We? 'Ask Travis Hanlon.'

'Travis?'

'Yes, I gave it to his father, Mick.'

'Why?'

'Because he removed it for me. And Travis helped him.'

'You sold it?'

'No, I gave it to him. His mother apparently was a stalwart of the congregation. It seemed appropriate.'

'Like a memento?'

'You could see it like that.'

'Well, that could be a problem. Travis wants to study acting when he leaves school and his dad will have a fit when he finds out.'

Now it's Zoe's turn to be surprised. 'Travis?' The surly boy whose voice rarely rises above a mumble?

'Yeah, Travis. You'll see.' And she looks around her with that air she has always of prosecuting a hidden agenda. Except that Melanie is anything but secretive, indeed she is blunt to the point of offence. And then, 'Do you know if Mick's still got the font?' *I must have the church. I will psych her into it. She will see that it's necessary.*

'No idea. He said it would make a good birdbath.'

'I'll give him a ring.' She grins again. 'Travis is playing the lead. That could be a plus. In the short term, anyway.'

'Travis is the *lead?*'

'Yeah, he's the Advocate. Didn't you see him at the rehearsal?'

'It wasn't obvious.' She was unable to tell then who was or wasn't anyone. And in any case, it had all been gibberish. 'It was quite a business to remove the font—it took the best part of a day. I doubt if Mick would want to go to the trouble of bringing it back and then removing it again.'

'We'll see.'

We'll see? Will *we*, Melanie?

She cannot deny that she enjoys this young woman's company: her determination, her brash optimism, her belief that she can get what she wants because, after all, she has an admirable purpose so why would anyone of even half-hearted goodwill want to thwart her? It reminds Zoe of someone, and that someone is Nick.

'What do you think of my stained-glass windows, Melanie?'

'They're good. Atmospheric. Good colour, good, filtered light. Better than a painted flat or a back cloth.'

Of course, everything is grist to her mill.

'I can offer you a sandwich.'

'Nah, thanks, gotta go.'

They walk out onto the steps of the church. Melanie stops and looks out to the side paddock, where sheep are grazing. 'McAlister's sheep, right?'

'Yes. You know him?'

'I know his daughter, Lily.'

'Really? How?'

'Friend of a friend. We moved in the same circles for a

while, in town before I came here. Heard she had a break-down over some bloke. Something bad happened and it was all hushed up. Lives at home now with her dad, has done for over a year. Can't seem to get it together. Sad. I tried to make contact, ask her out for a drink, introduce her to a few people. Rang McAlister but he didn't want to know.'

Zoe finds the idea unsettling, a young woman in retreat on that vast estate. 'He came here just after I arrived. Wanted a family plaque that commemorated his great-uncle.'

'What are you going to do with the rest of them, the plaques?'

'I haven't the faintest idea. One of many decisions I have to make and not at the top of my list right now.'

'I bet they thought when they put them up they'd be there forever.' Melanie grins. 'Nothing lasts, does it?'

'Some things, Melanie. Some things.'

But Melanie is striding across to her ute, as if she has remembered that she is due elsewhere; and this is characteristic of her, Zoe observes, these sudden moves, and she lingers on the steps of the church to wave her off, looking on with mild amusement as the Colorado disappears through the iron gates, which Melanie had left open on her arrival and which she will not bother to close.

By now it's almost seven in the evening and the light is beginning to soften. Zoe makes herself a sandwich and settles in front of the television, but in less than an hour the banality of it makes her restless. Perhaps she will go for a walk. No, she is not in the mood. What, then?

She begins to pace around the perimeter of the nave, thinking she might ring Isobel, and then she spots the script, perched on a pile of books on the altar. And, recalling the rehearsal in the gym, asks herself: could it really have been that bad?

She retrieves it now from its dusty pile (she really must put a dust cover over the books) and carries it to the dining area, where she spreads it out on the table because it's heavy and bound in one of those awkward spiral binds that won't sit comfortably on her knee. She opens it (at least it won't be predictable), half-expecting it to have a kind of zany energy, maybe even a kind of comic brio (there had after all been a glimmer of that in the drab gym rehearsal). And for the first time she wishes that Nick was there in the church with her. She could read it aloud to him and they would share the joke, and in the laughter those other things might dissolve, or at least blur around the edges. No, impossible. What a maudlin thought.

Melanie's precis is printed out in bold type. 'You need to understand, Zoe'—that familiarity again—'that this is not your conventional three-acter. There are no acts and it runs without an interval. It was written in 1901 but it's timeless. It doesn't aim to be realistic, anything but, it's meant to be like a dream, the way a dream is a mixture of things that come and go and one thing turns into another for no obvious reason. But if you get the pace right it runs like a song and if you get the visuals right it makes its own sense.

'Anyway, on to the plot. It starts with Indra, the ruler of the heavens, who's fed up with listening to the cries and moans of people on earth, so he sends his daughter down to find out why there is so much suffering going on. It's like: what's wrong with these earthlings? His daughter has to take human form which she does, along with the name of Agnes ("lamb of God"). This means she has to suffer herself. Think you see a Christ figure in female form? Well, yes and no. She doesn't get nailed to a piece of wood but she does suffer, including as the beaten wife of the character known as the Advocate, a lawyer who has to represent criminals and who is driven to despair by their crimes and takes it out on her.

'He's one of three main male characters: the Officer, the Advocate and the Poet. I've got three good boys but Travis Hanlon is the best of them. There are forty characters in all and they're all played by ten actors. Agnes is a big part and I've followed a production in Edinburgh in 1973 by dividing Agnes into three. It's too big a part for one young actor to carry and I've got three strong girls who share the dialogue between them. I'll dress them in white Grecian robes and they'll combine like a kind of female chorus.

'What follows is a parade of random events and there's a lot of stuff about a closed door. The characters are always wondering what's behind it and waiting for it to open but it never does. The answer to human suffering is behind the door but they can't get the door open. It's pretty hectic, a bit of a circus. Eventually Agnes returns to the heavens, exhausted but with a greater understanding of human suffering and compassion for the miserable sods below.

'All through the performance the image of a castle is projected onto a big screen behind the actors and gradually the castle grows and grows until at the end it catches alight. While it burns Agnes returns to heaven, leaving her human body behind to incinerate in the fire. The castle is a symbol of the world as a prison, only, as I've explained to the cast, it's what we choose to imprison ourselves in, and they get that, that we have a choice. But, anyway, at the end a giant chrysanthemum rises from the castle flames. We'll do that with digital images enlarged. So it's an upbeat ending.'

Upbeat? She must be kidding.

'Please read the script but remember you have to see it acted out and hear the words spoken.'

Well, she thinks, *Grease* it isn't. Again she thinks of Nick, who would approve. *Be ambitious: go for broke.* She gets up to fetch a glass of wine and then, setting Melanie's precis to one side, opens the script.

An hour later she pushes it away from her, her mouth open in a silent gasp of dismay. Melanie cannot be serious. What are a group of rural parents going to make of this, even if it should be done well? And what could 'well' possibly mean? There is no sense to it; it is a chaotic melange of anger, hysteria and confusion, fragmented and incoherent. This Strindberg must have been a madman. She feels sorry for Melanie now, for her failed ambition, her overreach. This will go badly, she says to herself; she will be abused, her confidence will be shaken if not destroyed, the young actors will be teased and mocked.

And a giant chrysanthemum! She never did like 'chryssies', as the women of her childhood called them. She recalls her mother dragging her and Isobel to a flower show in the town hall after a shopping expedition in the city, the price they had to pay for new clothes. In the hall there were dozens and dozens of single blooms, mostly in pastel shades of pink and apricot or a claret colour. They stood in narrow vases set on long trestle tables that ran the length of the room and there was an elderly man, leaning over a giant pink bloom and fussing at it with a long pencil, using the tip of the pencil to separate out its hundreds of petals and arrange them into a state of perfection.

Isobel had stared at him and smirked, and their mother had frowned and beckoned them away. 'That man is a champion grower,' she had said, crossly, and this had only provoked an outburst of giggles as Isobel rolled her eyes at Zoe. For a time, 'he's a champion grower' had become a catchphrase for them, part of their private language of female mockery.

But what to do about Melanie? The cast must not come to the church and she will tell Melanie so. But she must convey her decision as diplomatically as possible; she will not comment on the play but refer only to her own privacy, a not unreasonable consideration. She will give Melanie a good dinner and say she is uncomfortable with the whole idea and she is sorry but that's how it is, and she will offer to make a contribution to the expenses of mounting the play, perhaps even of hiring another venue (though the Crannock community hall is dismal).

She is being weak; she does not want to be an accessory to Melanie's shame, and she should not feel bad about this because she owes Melanie nothing. In the morning she will text Melanie and suggest dinner on Friday evening. Something special. She will defrost the deer casserole.

25

At six-thirty on the Friday she hears the distinctive sound of the Colorado ute coming up her drive. She has set the table with care and brought in flowers, expensive peony roses. She has lit some of Lachie's candles. None of this will soften the blow.

Melanie, it turns out, is ravenous. 'This deer is wonderful. I might have known you'd be a good cook.'

Ah, yes, that performative skill of the privileged that she has all but abandoned.

Melanie sighs. 'When I come home, I'm too tired to cook. I live on tofu wraps.'

'Are you vegetarian?'

'Sort of.'

'Can you be a sort-of vegetarian?'

'Is this a test of my moral fibre?'

'Absolutely. How about we test it further with dessert?'

In the little kitchen she bends to extract the coffee ice-cream from the freezer and feels a momentary pang. She must steady her nerve. She must sever the connection as painlessly as possible.

Melanie lifts a spoonful of the ice-cream to her lips and puts it back down again. She comes to the point. 'You've read the script?'

'Did it ever occur to you, Melanie, that you were taking a risk in giving it to me?'

'No.'

'I found it incomprehensible.'

'You'll be surprised.'

'Surprised by what?'

'When you see it spoken by actors. You can't read a play. Words need to be embodied.'

She thinks of Nick's letter to the girl: sometimes words are more potent on the page.

'I saw your rehearsal. It made no sense to me at all.'

'Work in progress.'

'Why do you want to do it? I looked it up on Google and people seem to think it's unstageable, even using professionals.'

'I don't believe that. I've watched productions on YouTube and the actors are too old. You need the innocence of kids.'

'You think they're innocent? I'm sure they torment one another.'

'You bet they do. But they're not jaded.'

She doesn't say that what she had seen in the school gym was an ugly shambles, but neither can she entirely contain her scepticism. 'Do you really think they understand what they're saying? If I as an adult found it hard to follow, then what could they possibly make of it?'

'Of course they understand it. They understand it the way you understand anything. You breathe it in.'

It's a point so obscure that Zoe chooses to ignore it. She turns instead to practicalities. 'There's a castle at the end that catches fire and turns into a giant chrysanthemum.'

'The castle is the prison of the world.'

'And the chrysanthemum?'

'The chrysanthemum is the release of the soul.'

'So you believe in the soul, Melanie?'

'Not exactly.'

'Not exactly?'

Melanie casts a dismissive glance up at the windows. 'Not in the way this lot do.'

'I see. So, the fire, the chrysanthemum. How are you going to do that?'

'Easy. Digital effects. I've got Tyler in charge of that, a kid in the industrial-design class. He'll come up with the images and we'll project them onto a big screen.'

Melanie, she observes, is nervous. Perhaps she senses what is coming. Don't weaken, she tells herself, get it over with—at which point her mobile buzzes. It's Dominic. Dominic, who rarely ever calls! 'I'll have to take this for a minute,' she says and carries the phone into the kitchen. 'Can I call you back?' she asks. 'Give me an hour.'

On the table Melanie's ice-cream is melting into a shallow pool. 'Sorry, that was my son. I wouldn't have answered otherwise. I'll ring him later.'

'How many children have you got, Zoe?'

'Two. Young men now.'

'Are you divorced?'

'My husband is dead.'

'I was married once.'

'Really?'

'Yeah, when I was twenty-four.'

'So I take it you're divorced?'

'No.' Melanie holds her gaze. 'He drowned.'

'Oh, no.'

'Oh, yes. We went away for a weekend to the coast. Great weather, off to the beach in the morning.' So matter-of-fact. 'I fell asleep on the sand. He got caught in a rip. I woke up and he wasn't there. They found him eventually. All cut up on the rocks. Washed up when the tide turned.'

'How long ago was this?'

'Two years next month.'

'Was he an actor?'

'Robbie? No, he was better than that. He was a cabinetmaker. He taught me how to use tools.' She pauses. 'He was good-looking too. I'm not, I know. I don't know what he saw in me.' She pushes the dish of melted ice-cream away from her. 'Sorry, I can't eat that.'

Zoe looks up at the window opposite: St Martin in his plumed helmet, wielding his long sword. *Only one cloak and so much pain.* When she turns back towards Melanie the young woman is staring at her, and perhaps sensing that she has the advantage, she takes it. 'I think the kids would be ready to do a trial run here in around a fortnight.'

'A trial run?'

'Well, it would be good if we could actually mount the performance here, but if not we could at least put on a special performance for you.'

She has made the leap and her nerve is breathtaking.

'I'll think about that, Melanie. But you *can* rehearse here.' She pauses. 'For the acoustics.'

'Thanks. You won't regret it.' Melanie pushes her chair back and stands. 'To be honest, I'm cooked. It's been a long week.'

She walks Melanie to the door and as the ute turns onto the road she takes out her phone to ring Dominic. He does not answer.

26

Her old friend Helen Bury rings to invite her to a dinner to celebrate Leo's birthday. Her first impulse is to make her excuses; she has not been to the city since moving into the church, has had no reason to and felt no desire to leave the valley. The Burys have twice announced they are coming to visit her in Crannock 'to see your lovely little church' and both times, to her relief, they have had reasons to postpone. But, as it happens, Zoe is booked for a breast screening in the city on the day of Leo's birthday. Her old fondness for Helen surfaces and she hears herself say: 'Well, I could drop by for an hour or so but I'm afraid I couldn't stay.'

'At least come for a drink. I have something for you.'

Just after two she parks outside Helen and Leo's handsome Victorian terrace in a wide street lined with plane trees. Helen must have seen her car pull up, for she flings open the door and rushes to the gate to embrace her. 'My dear girl, you've been a stranger. It's so good to see you.'

They sit outside on the rear terrace, shaded by vines, and look out into a long and narrow courtyard. Its high brick walls are lined with topiary, huge terracotta urns planted with spindly trees, their tall trunks rising into dense, leafy heads that have been cut into neat spheres. Beside her glass of chilled white wine Helen has laid a large manila envelope, and when she feels they are settled she pushes it across the glass-topped table to Zoe. 'For you.'

'What's this?'

'I was sorting through files of photos the other day and I found some lovely ones of the four of us at Blackheath, that time when we rented the bush cabin. I've had them printed out for you.'

'Oh.'

'Nick was in such good form that weekend.' Helen sighs. 'Everything was more fun when he was around. It was the last time we saw him.'

'No. We came over one night, not long after. To see the new movie room.'

'Oh, that. I'd forgotten.'

Zoe removes the envelope from the table and drops it into her handbag. 'Do you mind, Hel, if I don't look at these now?'

'Of course not.' Helen assumes a grave face. 'Of course not—too soon.' And then, hastily: 'Look, why not stay the night? Leo would love to see you. He'll be home by seven.'

'I'd like to, Hel, but I can't. I have something on at the weekend and I need to get back tonight. Tell Leo I'm sorry. Next time.' It is in part a feint, but she does have something on at the weekend: Melanie and her troupe of players.

Helen is leaning across the table to top up her glass. 'Is there much social life where you are?'

'Enough. Enough for me.' Her friend, Zoe observes, is flushed and looking tight around the eyes. 'How are you, Hel? How have things been?'

'Well, to tell you the truth, not all that good. We love this place, as you know, we've been here years, long before it became fashionable, but everything's changing. That house next door, a worker's cottage for heaven's sake, has been tarted up with a huge extension. Cost a bomb.'

'I noticed.'

'A heritage façade at the front, all prettified, and ripped the guts out of the interior. Which was fair enough, because it was dark and full of mould. But now a brutal black cube on the back.' She stares gloomily at the monstrosity next door, looming above the courtyard wall as if to keep her modest topiary under surveillance. 'The most schizophrenic building I've ever seen.'

'It must have been noisy.'

'It was. Weeks and weeks of it. You've no idea. And just when we thought they'd finished, it started up again. A plunge pool! We're on sandstone bedrock here, as you know, and they had to drill directly into it. The whole place shook. Our courtyard walls cracked from the jack-hammering and plaster fell off the walls upstairs above the staircase. We've only just had them repaired. All this on top of the couple opposite excavating a two-storey under-ground carpark. It's been a nightmare.'

'Did you complain?'

'No point. They had council permission. But we won't be inviting them in for drinks.'

'I suppose not.' *You won't be inviting them over for a night in the movie room*, Zoe thinks, and then rebukes herself: *You sound just like Nick*. In that moment she can hear his voice, deep and resonant, so clear, so close to her ear, and it's as if some solid object, long tethered in her chest, is unmoored and she is cast adrift on a tide of abject yearning.

Helen is looking wistful. 'I envy you your peace in the country.'

'No, you don't—you'd hate it.'

'Are you crying?'

'Only at the idea of you in the country.'

'Well, *you* seem to like it.'

'I have reasons to.'

'Of course. There I go, being tactless again.'

'It's fine, it really is.' She reaches across the table to take Helen's hand. 'It's been good to see you, Hel, really good. Just what I needed. But I must go if I'm to avoid the traffic. I'm not used to it now.' Still on a precipice of tears, she stands and, with her back to Helen, walks to the edge of the terrace. 'I like your trees, Hel. They're so... so orderly.'

'Well, Leo's a control freak, as you know. But they *are* pretty. Sort of Tuscan. We thought of lemon trees but...' She shrugs. 'they're so temperamental.'

Good old Helen, so practical, so not at all temperamental.

'We'd love to come down and stay for a weekend. Let me know a good place and we'll book in. You know how fussy Leo is.'

The traffic is slow and bumper-to-bumper. She stayed too long, and regrets the second glass of wine. Mercifully the rush of disorientation she experienced in the Burys' courtyard, the sickly bloom of nostalgia, is beginning to fade. Focusing on the long line of cars ahead, a row of metallic beetles gleaming in the late-afternoon sun, she waits for her exit onto the freeway and contemplates the weekend. Tomorrow she will clean the church and early on Sunday evening Melanie and her motley crew will arrive.

The drive back to Crannock is tiring, a procession of weekenders escaping to the southern end of the valley where the vineyards are. It's dark when she unlocks the door of the church and steps into the empty vestibule, into the familiar smell of incense and stone dust.

She can't be bothered with dinner, and eats a supper of biscuits and cheese in front of the seven o'clock news. After the weather forecast (still no sign of rain) she attempts to read but the words on the page resist her will to absorb them. Unable to focus, instead she takes a long shower, the lukewarm water flowing over her head in a steady stream while random thoughts scroll across her mind's eye. What were the trees in Helen's courtyard? She had meant to ask.

How vulnerable they looked in their manicured precision, how brittle. What will she buy at the market tomorrow for Sunday night's supper? It's such a long time since she had to cater for adolescents and several of them are bound to be vegetarian, especially the girls. And what will these young players make of St Martin's? For some, Melanie had said, it will be their first time inside a church (and there's an arresting thought). How will they know where to stand, where to move, and will they be in costume? She hadn't thought to ask. Will the acoustics make a difference, or will it be a mumbling farce so that she will have to fake her compliments?

She steps out onto the bathmat in that lucent interval when, after a shower, she is naked and shiny wet in the nave as if born again (her little joke), and she wraps a towel around her head. Then to the kitchen where she plugs the hairdryer into the power point that serves the toaster and the electric kettle. Still improvising, she thinks, still making do, still without plans for a plunge pool.

Hair dry, she checks the deadlock on the church door, turns out the main light that illuminates the fake candles on the chandelier and carries her handbag to beside the bed. There, rummaging in the bag for her phone, her fingers pluck at the manila envelope of photographs. She hesitates, resting it on her knee. Then, rising from the bed, she carries it to behind the reredos at the rear of the altar where she drops it into the box marked THE CONVERSION.

27

So they come on the Sunday evening, a night when none of them is working in a fast-food outlet or stacking shelves in one of the local supermarkets. Zoe has prepared supper: cheeses and dips and bowls of potato chips and a large chocolate cake. Melanie has instructed them to wear costume, which turns out to be, in most cases, black jeans and T-shirts or black jackets borrowed from a father or older brother, and white shirts with black shoes ('no sneakers'). Travis Hanlon appears in the doorway in a black Metallica T-shirt with a bejewelled skull on it, already with a different aura about him than the silent youth who had helped his father to remove the font.

Melanie slaps him on the back. 'Get that off,' she says, and he grins and changes into a plain white long-sleeved cotton shirt from a batch that Melanie has bought at an op-shop.

Zoe is introduced to the three girls who are to play Agnes, Lamb of God. Gemma, Sky Lee and Ellie. And finds she is staring at Ellie, who looks familiar: the long nose, the tilt of the head, even the curve of the chin. They have never met but something about this girl brings on a shiver of unease. The girls are smiling, and say thanks so much for having us, and is there somewhere they can change? And she nods, and says, 'Of course,' and leads them to the kitchen, Melanie following behind with a large garbage bag of costumes.

Some twenty minutes later they emerge with their hair wound up in an old-fashioned chignon and their bodies draped in a classical Grecian tunic that exposes one shoulder and falls to the floor in long white folds (these have been sewn by Melanie). The effect of the chignon is startling; it confers an instant dignity on the girls, and while only one of them is conventionally pretty they all have a natural presence. She can see why Melanie has chosen them.

Melanie had arrived in the afternoon with four of the boys and they brought with them a stone birdbath on a plinth that Melanie had found in the backyard of an antique shop. It was too low, Melanie said, and she had 'knocked up' a strong box of hardwood for it to stand on. The box is painted bright green. Mick Hanlon had not unreasonably declined to return the font but Melanie is bent on an imitation of it for a reason that is not clear to Zoe. Melanie asks now for a jug or a pot so she can fill the birdbath with water. Zoe produces a big yellow ceramic jug shaped like a pitcher and Melanie beams: 'Perfect!' By this time Zoe has given up all resistance and decided to deport herself with an air of mild amusement. As long as nothing is damaged...

Melanie and what she refers to as her set-up crew have cleared the books from the altar and draped the reredos with white gauze, and, using the same big roll that she imagines Melanie has bought from a fabric outlet, they conceal the shower alcove and the lavatory. But apart from this filmy minimalism, as far as she can see there are to be no props. Or rather, as she will discover, the props are already in place and they are hers.

You'll see. I'll show you what it could be like. Your own private performance.

Of course, they have no theatrical lighting. Melanie dims the lights in the iron chandelier and switches on the table lamps so they have a half-light along with a plethora of candles that the crew places around the church. Melanie has also acquired two wrought-iron candle stands of around two metres high, each stand having holders for a dozen thick candles. There are to be no special effects, no burning castle or giant chrysanthemum, because these as yet are not ready. If, Melanie explains, there were ultimately to be a performance in the church, the crew would erect a big screen above the altar. Tyler would project the image of the castle onto it, and at the end superimpose a second image of it going up in flames, and the giant chrysanthemum rising up out of the ashes. 'I saw his work-up yesterday and it's amazing,' she says. 'I'm just sorry we can't give you the full effect tonight.'

When everything is in place Melanie makes a show of directing the boys to lift one of Zoe's armchairs and place it at the centre of the nave, and then, clapping her hands in that brusque way she has, she calls the cast to take up their positions. A boy plugs a device into one of the power points and a harsh, discordant music begins to seep out from it, as if from the walls of the church, but the volume is low and after a minute or two it ebbs away, and a deep baritone rings out.

'Where are you, daughter, where?'

'Here, father, here!'

The three Agneses are deployed around the church. One sits on the altar; one stands in the pulpit; and the other stands on a small stepladder behind the birdbath—now a substitute font—holding the yellow pitcher and looking like a maiden from the bas-relief on a Grecian urn. The team has positioned an old door across the steps leading up to the pulpit, a door Zoe had last seen in the back of Melanie's ute and which has since been painted blood-red, and she guesses that this is to be the door in the play that is never to be opened, which must mean that the Agnes in the pulpit will be confined there for the duration.

And then it strikes her. The young cast has never been in the church before, never mind rehearsed here, and yet they knew where to place their props and where to take up their positions. Melanie has mapped out the space for them, has most likely given each actor a copy of the layout of the church and its fittings and instructed them to memorise it. She has taken care that the private performance for Zoe will have the maximum theatrical effect, so that Zoe will weaken and agree to the use of the church for the public performances.

I am being finessed.

The boy who is playing the father god, Indra, is tall and not bad-looking. She can see that he doesn't quite know what to do with his hands, but this is offset by the fact that he has a surprisingly good baritone, deep and resonant.

'You have lost your way, child. Take care, you are falling...

'Descend and see, and hear, and then return,

'And tell me, child, if their complaints and wailings are well founded.'

But the revelation is Travis Hanlon as the lawyer, the Advocate, who does not appear for some time, but as soon as he emerges from behind the reredos he commands the centre of the sanctuary with the authority of a demented angel. His black hair is oiled and slicked back and his dark eyes catch the light.

'Look at me. No-one ever comes here who laughs. Only hard glances, bared teeth, clenched fists. And they all spray their malice, their envy, their suspicions, over me...I can never wear clothes for more than one or two days, because they stink of other men's crimes.'

When, months later, she looks back on this evening she will not be able to recall any of the dialogue, not even a word. And yet something happens, something that creeps up on her until she is captured in a spell that has no name and no form, only a beguiling resonance that plays on her like a muted instrument, unknown and yet familiar. For weeks afterwards she will have flashbacks: the image of Travis Hanlon standing on the steps of the altar with a look of fury, his right arm flung out in a gesture of anguish.

'Look at these documents on which I write accounts of injustices…And do you think anyone wants to be friends with a man who must collect all the city's debts?'

Nothing about his performance is histrionic; every moment of it, every word and gesture, seems to emanate from him with a conviction she would have found barely credible if it had been described to her by a third party under other circumstances.

She understands then why Melanie had wanted the church, had been prepared to hound her for it. Within its walls the young actors are enlarged. The church confers on them an aura and instinctively they open themselves to it as if assuming a garment they have worn before in some other life, a garment that is natural to them, and familiar. The Grecian tunics of the Agnes trinity would look ridiculous in the school gym; here they are on the same plane as the carved wooden chalices on the reredos and the figures in the stained glass. The voices that had mumbled in the echoing gym here have a clarity that resonates in the nave and carries to the back wall.

Zoe glances across at Melanie, who is perched on a kitchen stool and making notes on a thick pad. Melanie does not look rapt; she looks like an artisan at work.

Finally, the three Agneses come together, side by side on the steps of the altar, to declaim their shared monologue before they return to heaven, and it's now that she sees who it is that Ellie reminds her of, for the resemblance is uncanny. And there she is, the girl, for the three have morphed into four and Sophie is standing between them. *No, it can't be.* She leans forward in her chair as if to get a closer look, half squinting at the tableau on the altar steps. Yes, it's her, looking as if she had been there all along, and in the hectic movement of the young cast, and the shouting, Zoe had somehow failed to see her.

And now the girl is speaking. 'You have abandoned me,' Zoe hears her cry, 'you have not cared what has become of me—'

Zoe closes her eyes. *It has come to this. I am hallucinating. Just when I thought I had escaped...*

The voices of the young women are blending now in a sonorous wave of sound that rises to a pitch of lamentation. 'Every joy that you have brings grief to others, but your grief brings joy to none...'

No, she thinks, *no, you don't understand. It's not that simple.* With a sharp intake of breath she opens her eyes, but the girl is no longer among them. The girl is nowhere.

The first Agnes, meanwhile, has moved to the top step of the altar and is making her farewell. 'Oh, now I feel the agony of existence! So this is to be mortal...One wants to go and one wants to stay. The twin halves of the heart are wrenched asunder...'

Zoe lowers her head and presses the thumb and fingers of her right hand against her eyelids. *There will be no tears.* The walls of the church have dissolved into a blur, but there is a voice beside her. It's Melanie.

'Well, what did you think?'

She does not look up but reaches for Melanie's hand. 'Give me a minute, Mel, and I'll bring out the supper.'

While they cluster in front of the sanctuary, sitting cross-legged on the fraying red carpet and listening to Melanie read from her notes, she is grateful for an excuse to retreat and busy herself in the kitchen. When at last Melanie dismisses them, they pack up and change into the clothes they came in. Over supper they laugh and talk and surreptitiously check their phones and in a fuzzily abstracted state she summons her congratulations and fragments of small talk and manages somehow to keep Melanie at a distance, saying: 'Let's talk about this in a few days. I've got a bit on my mind just now.'

'They're good, aren't they?' Melanie insists. 'I told you it would be different.'

More different than Melanie could know.

At the door to the vestibule she waves them off, by which time it is almost midnight and she is exhausted. For a long time she lies in her bed, stunned. *I have had a waking dream*, she tells herself; she had seen the girl plainly, in the same white Grecian folds as the others, and yet it was not possible. 'A waking dream,' she says again, this time out loud. Finally, she drifts off and for the next few hours dozes fitfully until, just as the early light begins to appear at the big windows, she falls into a deeper sleep and dreams again of the cathedral at Cologne.

This time there are just two people on the train, Zoe and Sophie, sitting beside the window in their enclosed cabin, racketing across a dark plain. Through the window they can see the cathedral ablaze, receding into the distance until its blackened towers are mere smudges on the horizon. Soon there will nothing left of it but ash, but it won't matter, for she knows now that she and the girl are bound together for the journey, and there is no longer anything to escape from.

28

Two weeks later, and she has ceded the church to Melanie, but does not trust herself to watch the play again. She will spend the first night of the two public performances in a motel.

At three in the afternoon of the opening night Melanie collects the spare key to the church from Zoe at the hospital and leaves with her team to set up the nave. Zoe stays on at the hospital until seven-thirty to deal with paperwork and eats at the Thai restaurant in the town, where she sits facing an embroidered silk hanging of Garuda, his golden talons locked onto a brass rod, his crimson wings spread wide.

Once outside, she finds she is not in the mood for the stuffy confines of her motel room. She gets into her car and heads for the back roads of the hills above the valley, and for ninety minutes drives beside the shadowy bush, encountering only the occasional flare of headlights and, mercifully, no wildlife. Just last week a woman had run into a big stag on this road and the stag had flipped onto the bonnet and shattered the windshield. Constable Cornes had been called and, after observing the beast's broken leg, had shot it. The woman was admitted to the hospital with a fractured sternum and facial cuts, and Zoe keeps this in mind as she navigates the blind corners. Some of these roads are rough and gravel stones kick up from her tyres threatening to strike her windscreen. Every now and then she passes a gate and a driveway that disappears into the bush, where the occasional house light glimmers between the blur of dense growth and the stars can be glimpsed through the canopy of the tallest trees. And all the while on the never-ending road her thoughts collide and blunt their edges on one another until they are weakened and fall away.

When, late at night, she returns to the church, she finds that they have cleared everything away, except for the big white screen set high above the altar. They have stacked the chairs brought in for the audience against the walls, and she had given them permission to leave her own furniture pushed back at the rear, where it remains. The nave is now an empty space.

On the evening of the second performance, she again sets out for the long, narrow road through the hills, listening to music and singing to herself, something she hasn't done in a long time.

When at last she returns to St Martin's, all is in order. They have even stacked her books back onto the altar. Though it is very still, some lingering sense of presence remains. On the dining table is a case of the valley champagne and a huge bunch of peony roses. There is a giant card standing upright, one of those cards for special occasions with balloons on the front, and inside it has been signed by the cast. Next to it is a note:

Thank you, Zoe. Now they know what they can do. Melanie.
PS The kids had a whip-round for the flowers.

29

A difficult day. Yet another locum has departed and there is no imminent replacement. Dr Khalid is overworked; frustrated callers trying to make appointments are abusive while Zoe attempts to pacify them. There are tears at the other end of the phone. The nurses on roster apply black humour to the situation; they are with few exceptions older women who have seen a great deal and are rarely fazed. There are two male nurses, also older. Darryl, a burly veteran with a small farm, occasionally brings her a bag of vegetables from his garden. Despite the daily frustrations, which are systemic, she has begun to feel at ease in the hospital, for the little building has a cheerfulness and a homeliness that big hospitals lack. When she locks up her office she is in good spirits. But tonight, as soon as she opens the back door of the hospital, she can smell the smoke. As she walks to her car she looks to the hills and then down into the valley, but there is no plume. Perhaps somewhere nearby a house has caught alight.

Ten minutes past the town she sees the roadblock. The smoke is thicker now and she knows that somewhere the bush is burning: she knows that smell. She is eighth in a line of cars, and a policeman comes to her window. 'I'm sorry, madam,' he says, 'but I'll have to ask you to turn around. It's not safe to go any further.'

'Where?' she asks.

'Where what?'

'Where is the fire?'

'On the McAlister property. They think they can contain it but we have to apply caution.'

Yes, caution: the valley is tinder. They had thought a major fire might come in January when Lachie visited and there had been a blaze in the national park but that had burned itself out. Now this. The church will burn, she tells herself, as if she has known it all along, known it at some deep level. Why else has she never been able to apply herself to the conversion? And when she had sold up in the city she brought the minimum of possessions with her, and little that she was attached to. And she has backed up the contents of her laptop. They exist in the cloud as well as on a memory stick she keeps in a drawer of her office at the hospital, along with photocopies of important documents. I am insured, she tells herself. And the thought comes to her: at last she will be free.

On the other side of town, close to the hospital, she books into a motel and drives off to collect Thai takeaway. In her room she eats her supper in front of the television news but the coverage is perfunctory: in the scale of things that in recent years they have become accustomed to, this is not one of the big fires. Then, just after nine, she receives a call from Constable Cornes, whose voice seems to come from a long way away. Good news, Mrs North, the church is fine, the church has not burned. There will probably be smoke damage to the interior so she is to prepare herself for a bit of a mess, but so far, so good.

So far, so good?

In the shower bay she stands for a long time, taking the force of the lukewarm water on her shoulders, her wet head bent forward against the glass wall of the enclosure to drown all thought. Stepping out into the cramped bathroom, naked and wet, she rummages in her toiletries bag to extract a sleeping pill. This night, of all nights, she will spend in the no-thought zone.

In the morning, before breakfast, she rings the police station: can she drive through to the church? No, not yet. Terribly sorry. The fire has been contained but the air is toxic and the ground still warm. We can understand how you feel, Mrs North, but we have to err on the side of caution.

Yes, absolutely, caution.

But on the following evening, just after dark, she is given clearance. She will go the next day.

It's after seven when she parks on the blackened verge in front of the big iron gates. She looks up to the top of the rise and there it is, the great survivor. I might have known, she thinks, but as she opens the car door she hears a shout from the graveyard. She looks over to where the unruly, overgrown bushes in the yard have been stripped bare by the fire, so that that the worn and lichen-encrusted head-stones are exposed. A dishevelled man in a baseball cap is swatting at the charred bushes with a cricket bat, as if beating birds out of a fruit tree, stumbling on the uneven ground and waving the bat with one arm, flailing.

She climbs out of the car and stands motionless on the verge, looking across to where, gripping the bat with both hands, he begins with a furious sweep of his outstretched arms to smash it against one of the more upright head-stones. 'Mongrel!' he shouts, glaring at the headstone and thwacking it with an agile fury. 'You mongrel!'

Surely she knows him? Something about him is familiar, but then, in the course of her work she sees almost everyone who lives in the valley. She is not alarmed, and in the strangeness of the moment can only stare, absorbing the hollow knock-knock-knock of wood against stone, knock and again knock, reverberating in her head as if she is imag-ining it, has summoned the stranger from some dark space. But no, there he is, *thwack, thwack* against the headstone like a prisoner escaped from a crypt. *This place is purga-tory*, she thinks, *and I have served my time*. And suddenly the stranger is done, has flung the bat into the charred bushes and is running down the hill towards the river. She waits until he is out of sight, then turns back to her gates, which are warm to the touch and covered in oily soot.

The grounds of the churchyard are black stubble,

littered with flamed-out embers. On three sides, McAlister's paddocks are blackened and the eucalypt plantation in the distance a charred ruin, line after straight line of desolate black trunks. And yet the solid door of the church had not caught, though its brass ring is, like the gates, warm to the touch.

Inside, the air is acrid, thick with the smell of burnt pine and eucalypt. She can feel her chest tighten and her eyes begin to smart. The ceiling and walls are stained with great smudges of smoke and soot, and a fine grey ash lies on every surface. It ought to look ugly and yet it's as if the essence of the space remains untouched. She should be dismayed but instead she sees in it a kind of ashen beauty: this place will always confound her.

She walks across the aisle to open the wardrobe and finds that her clothes reek of smoke. When she looks down, she sees that she has left scuffed footprints in the ash like marks made by a trespassing animal, and she is reminded of her first day in the church: the dead pigeon, scattered bird shit, possum scats on the fraying red carpet.

She crosses the aisle to her dining table and runs her fingers through the fine grey coating of ash on its surface; the ashen flowers in the vase are brittle and the pages of a book she had left open have curled crisply in the heat. Above her, the once luminous figures in the windows are smeary and dulled, the red of St Martin's cloak a burnt sepia. There is nothing to do but pack a small bag and return to the motel.

30

At the end of the week, in her lunch hour, she drives to the centre of town and walks to the realtor's office. Grant Ashton is there, seated at his desk and sipping on a styrofoam of coffee. When she enters he stands up, in the old-fashioned way. 'Mrs North. I'm so sorry to hear about the fire. What's the damage?'

'Not as bad as it might have been. It will need a professional clean but my insurance will pay for that.'

'Well, that's good to hear. Let me know if I can help in any way.'

'You can. You can put the property on the market.'

He looks startled, disapproving almost. 'I can understand how you feel—it must be a horrible sight out there —but...'

'But?'

'Well, you might feel differently in a few weeks' time. After it's all been cleaned up.'

No, she will not feel differently. It's not about the fire, it's about the ghost. And now the ghost has been set free.

'I can assure you, Grant, that I won't be changing my mind. Please list it.'

'I suppose you'll be needing a place to rent.'

'Gail McVilly has kindly offered me a chalet on her property that she keeps for visitors, until I can make other arrangements.'

And so it is that, as the cooler air of autumn rises in the valley, she moves into Gail's little chalet. The chalet has been used for short-term accommodation, but Gail has nominated a modest rent that in any case will be paid by the insurance company until the clean-up is completed. After that, Zoe will pay it herself while she decides where to live next.

The chalet reminds her of her grandmother's hop-picking hut, a two-room rectangle with vertical-board cladding painted a pale green. The varnish on the front door is cracked but the interior has been freshly painted and installed with new white blinds. Two old couches are draped in cream bedspreads printed with bold yellow daisies but the light into the living room is blocked by an old protea bush outside the window that has grown into a tree. The bed is new, though there is barely room on either side of it to move.

At weekends she sometimes sits outside on the park bench by the old cast-iron bath planted with marigolds and there she reads for an hour at a time, or simply gazes down at the olive pickers on the slopes. Gail tells her about a path through bushland on the other side of the main road that leads to the river, and here, beneath a feathery grey-green canopy of river wattles, she can sit and contemplate the crystal clarity of the water as it flows across the smooth river stones exposed by the drought, or eddies around rock pools in ripples that catch the sun. This is snake territory and in the heat she had avoided the river, but now is the best season of the year.

From time to time she leaves a message on Melanie Doyle's phone but there is no response. *So I was useful then and now I no longer am.*

31

The clean-up of St Martin's begins. A married couple in middle age turn up early one morning at the hospital and introduce themselves as Hedley and Patsy Burt. Both are covered in tattoos and Hedley has either lost his hair or shaved it. They set up a mobile home in the Crannock camping grounds, and it happens that Mick Hanlon knows them. When Zoe drops in on the Hanlons at the weekend hoping to see Travis and congratulate him on his performance, Mick tells her that Hedley is an old bikie who once worked as a rigger on building sites in the city. No problem for him to set up the scaffolding in the church, he says, so he can clean the ceiling and the upper reaches of the walls. He then ushers her out into the backyard to survey the damage from the fire: a singed paddock, a burnt-out chook house and a blackened shed. 'Lucky the fire truck turned up when it did,' says Mick. 'Trav was a big help, loaded the chooks into the ute and worked one of the hoses.'

They return to the kitchen, where Berenice has made a pot of tea and set out a plate of scones.

'Is Travis here?' Zoe asks.

'Trav's gone to town to see a play,' says Berenice, who has come up behind them. 'He's got the bug.'

Mick is chewing on a scone. 'No money in that,' he mumbles.

'Oh, I don't know. Russell Crowe's done all right.'

'Trav's no Russell Crowe.'

Berenice looks to Zoe. 'We'll see,' she says, and winks.

That wink again, and Zoe is attuned to it by now. That wink is how Berenice manages her world.

There is not always relief available for the reception desk, but on the Wednesday after the Burts arrive she is able to make an arrangement and she drives out to the church to look in on the clean-up. She takes with her a large thermos of coffee for the Burts, and some croissants and cheeses. The Burts have rigged up a spirit stove and are relaxing in camp chairs at the side of the church, reheating what Patsy says are leftovers from the night before. They offer her some of her own coffee, and Hedley demonstrates a new camping device they have for making fresh coffee and she laughs (she must ask Lachie if he owns one). For lunch they have made a pot of billy tea that stands steaming on a small fold-up wooden stool and Zoe is taken by their air of at-homeness, of relaxed self-sufficiency. She imagines them possessed of a cheerful accommodation to circumstance that they carry with them wherever they go.

Hedley is a giant of a man with a massive torso and square, blunt-fingered hands. The small and slender Patsy has a leathery face, the skin coarsened and lined in furrows. Her thin black hair is pulled back into a knot, but her lithe body in its cut-off shorts and skimpy singlet reveals good muscle tone and a set of square, bony shoulders up for work. There is something taut in the way she holds herself that suggests she might once have been a dancer. She is probably younger than she looks.

Hedley offers Zoe his chair, and, removing the billy, sets it down on the blackened earth before lowering himself onto the stool. 'Must be hard for you,' he says, 'to see it like this.'

'It is.'

'Easy for me to say but it could have been worse. A bigger fire would have blown your lovely windows out.'

Patsy grimaces. 'Trouble is, I can't get 'em clean. The soot's all sticky on 'em and none of the usual solvents work. Afraid you'll need to consult a specialist.'

Hedley blows at his tea to cool it. 'Yeah, still some people around who make stained glass. They'd know how to tackle it. But your insurance should cover that.' He grins. 'Not an item that's often claimed on, I'll bet.'

'Come and have a look,' says Patsy. 'I'll show you what I mean.'

They stand and walk to the church door, where they defer to her; it is after all her place and not theirs, though once inside they behave like tour guides, looking more at home in it than she does. It is now almost empty. Her wooden furniture is in storage, her table and dining chairs and her great sideboard, but anything upholstered was too smoke-ridden to bother with and she had arranged for it to be carted to the tip. And now the interior has sprouted a network of bamboo scaffolding that looks as if it might have grown out of the walls, and she sees that already they have vacuumed up most of the ash.

Patsy points to the window of St Martin. 'I like that one,' she says, 'it's a beauty. Good-lookin' fella, isn't he?' And she gives the hoarse cackle of the lifelong smoker. She points to the red cloak and explains how she has removed most of the surface grime but, try as she might, she cannot restore the full clarity and sheen of the colour. 'I've given it a red-hot go with the sodium peroxide, that usually does the trick.'

'Sounds drastic.'

'Horrible stuff. Need the protective gear for that.' And she points to the bottom of the scaffolding beneath the window, where a low plank is draped with a big overall, a set of goggles and elbow-length gloves. 'It's the bits around the solder that won't budge. They've got me beat.'

Hedley is behind them. 'I reckon you might have to take the windows out, take 'em to a workshop.' He sighs and she senses his disappointment that the windows have defeated them. 'Cost a bit. As I said, talk to your insurance guys. If they agreed to insure the place they must have calculated the risks.'

'You've done an amazing job.' For they have, and she is touched by the pride they take in giving back to her what she has lost. They are so pleased with their effort that she does not tell them she will not be moving back into the church. When the Burts have finished she will, on Mick Hanlon's advice, buy them a case of local gin and thank them profusely, all the while feeling detached, as if the church had never belonged to her, as indeed it never really has.

Outside again, she walks around to the eastern flank, where the old pines are stark trunks of charcoal with branches jutting out in blackened spikes above what's left of McAlister's electrified fence. Had it not been for the conflagration of the pines, the interior of the church might have been spared so much oily soot, though some of that must have come from the inferno of the eucalypt plantation. The pines had been planted by the early settlers and now the biggest of them is just a hollow stump that had smoked for days. They will not regenerate. No more black cockatoos.

Days later, when she drops a set of keys into Grant Ashton, he affects a mood of rueful pessimism. It's as if he is disappointed in her, that she is giving up too easily.

'Could take a while to sell,' he says, shaking his head. 'It's not exactly pretty out there, everything black—the ground, I mean. Trees all scorched. People looking for a tree change might not be up for it. Hardly scenic.' And he reminds her that it had taken a long time to sell it to her 'in its prime'.

'I can wait,' she says.

32

Gail is solicitous but not intrusive. Occasionally they share a meal, though each is careful not to presume on the other's privacy.

One weekend, Gail's nephew Simon comes to stay with his girlfriend, Holly. They are soon to be married and Gail has offered her property for the wedding ceremony. She, as a civil celebrant, will officiate.

Holly is a slender young woman with finely drawn features and a no-nonsense air. She is in her late twenties, Zoe guesses, and earnest in a girlish way. She and Simon met on a Tinder date they both describe as 'magical' while exchanging a brief smile of complicity, a lovers' smile, as if they alone have access to a secret knowledge beyond the understanding of others.

Simon explains that he had been flicking through profiles on Tinder when he got to Holly's. 'She said the two things she liked most were foreign movies and pinot grigio. I'd just been to a Korean movie and had a glass of pinot in my hand at the time and I thought: *That's got to be a good sign*. This epiphany had been almost twelve months ago and now they are finding it difficult to write the vows for their wedding. They don't want any soppy poems—'done to death'—so what does that leave? In the afternoon Gail had shown them a book she keeps, a collection of poems and quotations about love and union and, as Simon says, 'all that sort of thing', but they hadn't found anything there that 'spoke' to them.

Holly: 'I think the word *love* has been debased, don't you?'

Gail shrugs. 'Just say how you feel about one another,' she ventures.

'But that's the problem. There are no words to do it justice.'

'Well, there are more words in English than other languages, so you should be able to find some.'

'With respect, Gail, it's not that straightforward. We know how we feel but we need to find words that are…I don't know.' She gives a little laugh. 'Fresh.'

Simon puts his arm around her shoulder so that it flattens her long hair, and in an elegantly assertive gesture she raises the curtain of hair so that it lies free across his arm. 'Actually,' he says, 'Sanskrit has ninety-six words for love, far more than English. English has one.'

Gail smiles at him indulgently. 'Well, perhaps you could borrow a few.'

Zoe thinks of the retreat that Simon had come from the last time they met. Perhaps, she says, they could have a silent ceremony, no words at all. She isn't serious and instantly regrets her mocking tone but Holly gazes at her, wide-eyed and startled. 'That is *such* a good idea.'

Holly is returning serve, and fair enough.

'I don't see how that would work,' says Gail, with a sardonic lift of the eyebrows. 'There are legalities to be observed, for one thing.'

Simon persists in his earnestness, a quiet stubbornness that Zoe can't help but admire. 'Words are so important,' he says. 'If you have to have some, and they do, they must be the right ones or they will strike a false note.

Yes, a false note. A false note breaks the spell.

He refers then to the recent trouble in the States, where a priest had changed one word in the baptism service, as a result of which hundreds of children had not been legitimately baptised.

'I suppose that means that if they die they go straight to hell because of someone else's mistake.'

Zoe wonders if Gail is serious; with Gail it can be hard to tell. She thinks of the baptismal font that Mick Hanlon had removed from St Martin's and that stands now in a corner of his blackened shed. 'Had the offending priest failed to sprinkle the child with water?' she asks.

'No,' says Simon, who seems to have an interest in these things, 'the priest had merely said, "We baptise you"—meaning everyone present—instead of "I baptise you". He was trying to be inclusive.'

'Another case of good intentions gone awry,' says Gail.

'A leading theologian called it an example of

touchy-feely horizontalism,' says Simon.

'As opposed to what?'

'As opposed to the vertical authority transmitted downwards by God into the person of the priest.'

'I see, and where does that leave me?'

'You, Aunty Gail, are the authority of the horizontal.'

'Well, I'm glad to hear it, even if it does sound vaguely suggestive. But you still have to come up with a wedding service.'

Zoe thinks of St Martin's. That was my problem with the church, she could say: I couldn't conceive of a way to turn the vertical into the horizontal. 'As much as possible, vertical space (heaven) must be rendered horizontal (earth)'. But that would involve a long explanation, and in any case it was a red herring.

'The theologian said that the use of "we" meant the people there were worshipping themselves rather than God.'

'This seems to have piqued your interest, Simon. Is that why you are a Buddhist?'

'I'm not a Buddhist, Aunty, I just went to a retreat because I needed some space.'

Holly: 'What's the strangest wedding you've officiated at, Gail?'

'There've been a few. There was the Elvis wedding. There was the Mickey Mouse–themed wedding.'

'Seriously?'

'The bride and groom were Japanese. This was when

I was still living in Sydney. Then there was the older couple who had a Beatles wedding. They'd found a site online where you could buy Beatles wigs and they gave them out before the service for people to wear.'

'And did they?'

'Some did. It depended on whether you wanted to spoil your hairdo.' She laughs. 'They had a Beatles cover band for the reception and they were rather good.'

'A girlfriend of mine married an Indian guy last year in a Hindu temple. Instead of rings they garlanded one another and that was lovely. That was the ring moment, the moment when you become man and wife.'

'Well, you could garland one another,' says Gail. 'I think that's a lovely idea.'

And then there was a wedding they had both attend-ed recently where at a certain point in the service the wedding rings, in a little velvet pouch, had been passed around those present to handle so as to imbue them with 'positive vibes'.

Zoe wonders how you could guarantee that the vibes were positive but doesn't comment. Meanwhile, Gail is relating the story of a mother of the bride who had rung her from New York to ask what Gail would be wearing and whether it would 'tone in' with her own outfit. 'And that included her nail polish.'

'What did you say?'

'I have three outfits for weddings and I sent her photos of all three and let her choose. I made it plain that, beyond that, negotiations would not be entered into.'

Holly yawns. The young couple exchange a loving glance and rise from their chairs, declaring themselves tired and in need of an early night.

When they have disappeared into the house, Gail refills Zoe's glass. 'It's hard for them to have to make it up from scratch. My father was English and old-fashioned. He used to talk about good form. In his time everyone knew what the form was.' She fingers the rim of her empty glass. 'For better or for worse. And now we have to make it up as we go along.'

'I was married in an old-fashioned registry office,' says Zoe. 'We didn't have to make up anything. In those days it was that or a church. There were no celebrants and we couldn't bear the thought of a priest droning on.'

'And then you ended up buying one. A church, I mean.'

'Yes, though I always had mixed feelings.'

'Well, it's a lovely spot.'

'Yes, it is.'

'And I suppose if your husband were still alive you'd still be there.'

'Who knows?'

'It was very good of you to let the kids from the school do their play there.'

'You went?'

'Of course. I go every year. One has to support these things, and in any case I know these kids.'

'What did you think?'

'Well, this one was a bit different from previous years. I have to say I hadn't the faintest idea what it was about, but I was moved. The kids all looked so lovely. So serious.' She sighs. 'So lovely,' she says again. 'And a spectacular ending. The burning castle. The big lotus.'

'It was a chrysanthemum.'

'Was it? Hard to tell. The image was a bit blurry. I thought maybe a lotus.' She pours herself another glass of wine and settles back in her chair. 'What did *you* make of it?'

'I felt as you did. Melanie Doyle has a gift. I can only wonder what she'll do next.'

'She won't be doing anything. Not at the school, at least. She's resigned.'

'*Resigned*? Melanie?'

'Yes, out of the blue, apparently.'

'Really? I didn't know.' Why hadn't Melanie told her this herself? 'Gone to another school?'

'No, no. That's the thing. She just went off and joined that survivalist cult out the back of Beralga. You know, the one that breeds pigs and makes their own smallgoods. Word is they've built a big underground bunker for when the climate heats up.'

'End-of-the-world stuff?'

'Well, for us. Presumably not for them.'

'Tinned food and guns.'

'I don't know about the guns. They have a peace sign on the gates.'

'I had no idea Melanie was…' Zoe hesitates. She cannot find the words. The Melanie she knew was resolute, single-minded even, but not fanatical. 'Is this new?'

'I think they moved in around three years ago. Bought up an old farm and pooled their resources. I'm told that each member of the community has shares in the business. They seem to know what they're doing. They sell all their product into the city at top prices.'

'Melanie is breeding pigs? Melanie Doyle?'

'I gather it was something of a sudden conversion.'

'Is there a man involved?'

'No idea, but that would explain it if there were. Mind you, there was something about her…I wondered if she might be, you know, lesbian.'

'I don't think so. She was married once. To a man.'

'That doesn't mean anything these days. It sometimes takes a marriage to make you realise you don't want a man after all.'

It's an odd thing to say and Zoe wonders at Gail's past. And her own. She had wanted a man. She had wanted a man very much.

33

One evening in late May she gets a call from Grant
Ashton. 'Got a nibble,' he says. 'Young couple interested
in the church. Looking for a property to set up a restaurant. Inspecting on Saturday.'

'A restaurant? Seriously, Grant?'

'Yeah, think about it. Far enough out of town to
be a nice destination drive for city folk and close
enough for the locals if you want to have a drink with
your meal.'

'I see.'

Grant presses on. 'Definitely interested. Love the look
of the place. Cashed up and cock-eyed optimists. Grand
Designers, if you know what I mean.'

'And the price?'

'Let's see after Saturday. I wouldn't look a gift horse
in the mouth, Zoe.'

She is Zoe now. The prospect of two commissions
within six months has made her his intimate.

'They want to meet you. I've got an open home then,
though I'll try to get there before they leave. Otherwise,
we'll meet at my office later in the afternoon. Would be

good if you could show them through. But don't discuss money—wait until I get there.'

On the Saturday morning she drives up to the door of the church and unloads the car. She has brought with her a big vase and an even bigger bunch of bush flowers, and she arranges these in the vestibule on a small table, a rough outdoor fold-up she has borrowed from the chalet. She covers this with a brightly patterned cloth to conceal the table's splintery surface, and as she arranges the flowers she thinks of Isobel and her injunction to brighten the vestibule. And it's only possible for her to do so when she no longer has any investment in the place, other than to get the best price she can. It's all business now.

The young couple are late and she sits on the warm sandstone steps, her arms resting loosely on her knees. Eyes closed, she turns her face up to the sun and recalls the brown snake coiled on the top step when she and Nick had cruised up the drive on that first idle Sunday. She had been hostile, but Nick had been unperturbed, had not wanted to disturb it. During the parched summer months she had kept a wary eye out but had seen no sign of it, other than the rapid flick of a tail under the electrified fence one muggy afternoon.

At last she hears the sound of a car in the drive and stands, ready to greet her buyers. The young man introduces himself as Mark and he is handsome in a swarthy way, fashionably unshaven, and with a languid air he advances to shake her hand. Greta is more reserved. She stands back, and nods at Zoe with a patrician smile. It's clear who is in charge here.

Would they like first to inspect the exterior, she asks. She can point to the soundness of the walls and roof and explain the work done by the previous owner, unglamorous but reassuring. No, says Greta, they haven't got much time and would like first to look at the interior, to feel the vibe of the place.

As they stroll around inside, Mark says little, while Greta outlines their plans. Her sister, Mila, is a decorator and will be flying in from Basel in a fortnight's time. Should they decide to buy, they plan on a clean, modern look. 'Nothing rustic.'

'But the windows,' Zoe says.

'Oh, we've thought of that. We'd take them out. There's a stained-glass artist just outside Beralga. You probably know him.'

No, she doesn't.

'Stefan. Stefan Hennessey.' She pronounces his name with a rising inflection, as if surprised Zoe doesn't know this, and with the confident and mildly condescending air of one who is already in command. 'From the Hennessey hotel family. Mark went to school with him. Stefan would dismantle the pieces and reassemble them into abstract contemporary designs. We wouldn't want to lose them altogether—they give such a wonderful, filtered light. It's a feature of the place. We might even get nice colour patterns on the white tablecloths.'

Goodbye, St Martin. No shivering wretches will be dining here.

'I think you'll find that would be expensive.'

'Stefan has offered us a good deal. He's new in the area and it would be an advertisement for him.'

'So he's been here?'

'No need. Mark's given him the specifications.'

'Really?'

'He got the measurements from Grant. Approximate, of course.'

Mark has been wandering around alone, peering at the plaques. 'Depressing, aren't they?' he mutters, as if to himself. 'And ugly.'

'We heard you,' calls Greta, who by now is positively festive.

And he turns and laughs. 'Very fine acoustics,' he says. 'We'd have to do something about that. Have to install some baffles to muffle the carry. Diners don't want to hear each other's private conversations.'

Greta nods. 'Mila can deal with that.'

Relaxed and with hands in his pockets, Mark saunters across the nave to join them. He grins. 'What do you think, babe?'

He's so open, boyish even. But Greta is not about to give anything away. 'It definitely has possibilities,' she says. She turns to Zoe. 'We'll get back to Grant and see if we can arrive at an agreement.'

'Well, there's no hurry. You might want to think about it.' She knows Grant would wince at this if he were there but cannot help reacting to Greta's smugness.

In the vestibule Mark glances up at the old wall plaque with its lettering burnt into the wood: 'O Lord deliver us from our present fallen life.'

'That will have to go,' he says. 'We wouldn't want to give our customers the impression they're about to eat their last supper.'

34

The first to visit her in the chalet is Neville Glass.

'Don't bring any food,' she says, when he rings. 'The chalet is tiny. I've got two ancient hotplates and a microwave. We'll eat out.'

'At the church?'

'No, not this time. The fit-out is taking longer than anticipated.'

'As it always does.'

'Problems with installing the kitchen.'

'Have you seen the plan? It would be on the council website.'

'I gather they've removed just about everything except for the reredos. A perfect backdrop, they said. It has character. And grapes carved on it so, you know, appropriate.'

'Where are they putting the kitchen?'

'In the sanctuary. Where the altar was.'

'Of course.'

'They're planning to conceal it with a big lightweight screen that will drop from a bamboo rod suspended from the ceiling.'

'So you *have* looked at the plans.'

'Details like that are not on the plan but every now and then I run into the agent in town. Grant. He keeps me up-to-date. He takes a personal interest. A fancy restaurant, he says, is good for the town.'

'Do you miss it?'

'Not at all. Though I do keep seeing my big sideboard there, the only piece of me that looked as if it belonged.' She pauses. 'The only thing of mine that was grand enough.'

'Oh, I don't know. You can be pretty grand yourself.'

'Not lately.' Not ever.

In the days before Neville arrives, she prepares herself. He will stay at a local motel and after dinner at the Thai restaurant they will have a nightcap in the chalet. And then she will confront him. When he had visited before, she wasn't ready. Now she is.

They sit in a corner recess at a table with a thick plastic tablecloth in red and gold check. 'I come with news,' says Neville. 'I'm selling my apartment and buying a new townhouse. Just a block from where I am now.'

'Why?'

'Because it's got a fully enclosed internal courtyard and I've always wanted one.'

'But then it can't be a townhouse.'

'A new concept. Instead of going two or three storeys up, you build around the courtyard.'

'But your apartment had a lovely view.' Neville's apartment, bought with a legacy left by his aunt, had floor-to-ceiling windows and a view that stretched to the far horizon.

'This is a different kind of view. Instead of looking out, you look up. You have your own slice of the sky. And at ground level you have a perfect centre. So you have the horizontal and the vertical in perfect harmony.'

'Nick would have found that idea interesting.' She can speak of him now.

'He'd have said I was withdrawing.'

'Aren't you?'

'Not at all. I want to look up, not out. The conventional view has become a romantic cliché. And anyway, after a while you don't see it anymore, or you start to feel that the view is looking in on you.'

No wonder he and Nick understood one another. They could talk like this for hours. 'So you'll have your own piece of sky. Quarantined.'

He laughs. 'Ah, yes, but within the courtyard, every small change is a wonder. The merest movement of the clouds. The Chinese call it heaven's arch. I think the Chinese are right. If you narrow the view and look up, not out, you integrate heaven and earth.'

'But you don't believe in heaven.'

'It's a concept, dear Zoe.'

'Which works if you're Chinese.'

'You can adapt anything. We do it all the time. Look at you. Who could have imagined two years ago that you would be here?'

Yes, who could have imagined? 'And what will you put in this courtyard?'

'Some plants, maybe. A sculpture.'

'Your household gods?'

He grins. 'If I could figure out what they are.'

Enough of this talk, she thinks. 'Let's go back to my place for a nightcap.'

The bill is brought on a small brass tray with two mints in gold foil, and Neville picks up the docket and pockets the mints. Yes, she will let him pay.

In the chalet he settles on one of the old couches. Across her coffee table, which is too big for the chalet so that their knees press against the edges, she hands him his glass of whisky and soda.

'Where's my mint?'

He rummages in his pocket and produces one that he flips across the table to her. She opens it, slips it into her mouth and then proceeds to fold the gold foil wrapping into a tiny, neat square, as if the perfection of the edges is a matter of deep concern.

'Tell me, Nev, did you know about the girl?'

He freezes, glass halfway to mouth, and straightens his back. 'The girl?'

She sees then that he had known. 'Don't be coy, Nev. The girl, Sophie Crane.'

He lets out a long sigh and slumps back into the billow of the couch. 'Yes. Yes, I knew. We had a night out on the turps and he blurted it out. Sat in my car and cried.'

'And you said what?'

'Well, the obvious. That he was risking his professional status.'

'He was risking more than that.'

'Do you know, Zo, I don't think Nick ever wanted to grow old.'

'Don't change the subject, Nev. What did he tell you?'

He frowns and presses his lips together so that his mouth folds in on itself, as if he would apply his own gag. He does not want to go down this path and she shouldn't push it. It will come between them.

But push it she does. 'Well?'

'Well, that older man, younger woman thing, you know.'

'You're holding out on me, Nev.'

'He said he'd never known anyone like her. So open.'

'And?'

'And that her surrender—his words—her surrender was complete. Not in an impersonal way, as it was with some women.' He leans forward to peer into his glass as if there is something that doesn't belong there, a small dead insect perhaps. 'At a certain point in their pleasure you could be anyone. But with her...'

'Go on.'

'He said she offered herself in a spiritual way.'

Spiritual? The word nauseates her. 'Go on.'

'This isn't easy, Zo.'

'It's not meant to be.'

'He said…he said that when he was with her, he felt free.'

'Free of me?'

'No, not at all. He loved you. Free of the person Nick Wardlaw, a puppet of the gods.'

'Those were his words?'

'Yes.'

He is flushed now, and with a pained expression, but she is indifferent to his discomfort.

'Impersonal pleasure. Isn't that the best kind?'

'You know, Zo, I've always thought you were a pretty cool customer.'

'Is that a reproach, Neville?'

'Far from it.'

'You should have told me.'

'Why? He would have gotten over it and you could have gone on as you were. You were such a great couple. Who would want to spoil that?'

Poor Neville. She has hunted him down, and it will never be the same again.

In his own rueful way he would reproach her. 'Why haven't we had this conversation before?'

'Because neither of us was ready for it.'

He is silent. And then: 'So, what are you going to do now?'

'Lachie thinks I should buy a block of land and build a kit home.'

'Here?'

'Yes, here. It will take a while, of course. For one thing there's the problem of finding the right piece of land. There's the odd block available on low ground near the river but this is a flood plain. I need something a bit higher but that's harder to come by, and of course more expensive. Wherever I buy I'll only be able to afford a minimal build.'

'The church was in the ideal position, then.'

'Yes, that was its great selling point. And the price. Everything else was a problem.'

'So you'll stay in the valley?'

'I like this place. And I like my job. It's undemanding and I feel useful.'

'Ever thought of putting up your own shingle in the town?'

'No, thanks. I'd be a party to all the disputes in the valley. Before long I'd know all its unhappy secrets. Besides, I don't want to have to chase people for their debts.'

He asks now after Dominic, and she reaches for a notebook on the table and writes Dom's new details on a slip of paper. 'Give him a ring. He's fond of you. He always thought you were more fun than his father.'

'I could look him up when I next go to Melbourne.'

'Please. That is, if you're going soon. He rang me last week to say he is thinking of going to Vietnam. He's been offered work managing a bar in Da Nang.'

They are back on mundane ground, even if it now

feels loose underfoot. He hoists himself up from the couch and she accompanies him out onto the little deck, where he kisses her lightly on the cheek but does not attempt a hug. They are formal now with one another. From now on they always will be.

'Thanks for coming, Nev. Enjoy your slice of heaven.'

35

It's a Saturday morning and after she returns from the farmers' market she decides on a walk by the river.

The narrow track through scrub runs out to where a row of old English willows let down their branches to float on the surface of the water. Further along the bank is her favourite spot, a stand of river wattles beside a clump of dark green reeds.

But there are people here. Ten metres upstream from the track is a large rock that juts out into the river, and standing on it is a slender young woman in a floppy canvas hat, reflective sunglasses and a long, loose shirt over shorts. She is holding a fishing rod.

As Zoe draws closer, she sees that on the other side of the woman a stocky older man is standing in the water in waders. He has a small black fishing net hanging from his back, and despite the hat and reflective glasses she recognises him. It's Blair McAlister. Who, then, is the young woman? His daughter, perhaps, the one with the broken heart, the one that Melanie Doyle had tried to contact without success. *Messed up by a bloke*.

So intent are they on the river that they fail to register

her presence, and neither does she feel moved to declare it. She squats low to the ground on a grassy patch beneath one of the river wattles and hopes that they have been there awhile and will soon leave so that she will have the place to herself. But, instead, she begins to find herself lulled by the sunlit charm of their little tableau and especially the hypnotic repetition of their casting, the aerial dance of the long line above the water and the glittering lure of the fly.

The father is clearly an adept but the daughter a beginner; the motion of her arm is awkward and soon her line snags in a tree so that he must climb up from the shallows and onto the bank to untangle it. Once it is freed, he clambers up onto the rock and, taking her arm in slow motion, guides her casting action so that her next effort floats out over the water, lower and in a graceful loop. 'Let the fly drift down with the current,' she hears him say, 'like an insect on the surface. The trout will come up for it.'

She smiles; he pats her on the shoulder and then climbs down from the rock to wade back into the shallows, only now on the other side of the rock so that Zoe has a clearer view of him. The girl casts again but when she strips the line off the reel, the line over-spools. She hesitates, as if frozen, then with calm deliberation embarks on a patient rewind.

If the father has noticed this he does not comment. He has cast his line out over the water in a snaking roll, where the lure hovers on the surface like a mayfly.

Time now for Zoe to make her presence known, but before she can move there is a splash and a fish has raised its head above the water, open-mouthed, to take McAlister's hook. He raises his rod high until it's vertical and begins to thread the line in his left hand so that the fish is drawn in, squirming and splashing towards him. The girl laughs, looking down from her perch on the rock to where, after reaching behind him for the net, McAlister leans forward to scoop the shiny trout into its mesh. Deftly he unhooks the fish and, lifting it from the net, holds it aloft with both hands to show the girl, close enough for Zoe to see the fish's staring eye, its jaws working up and down. How perfect it is: the metallic glitter of its scales, the distinctive black spots and the slash of pink along its flank. Turning back to the river, McAlister bends low and, with one hand under the fish's belly and another on its tail, releases the trout into the water.

Back up on the bank he rummages in his tin box of flies and then, lifting his head, turns abruptly and, as if he has sensed her presence, looks across to where Zoe is sitting beneath the wattle, her knees pulled up to her chest. 'Mrs North?'

'Yes.' She stands and brushes the dirt from her jeans.

'Ah.' He is clearly taken aback.

She too is a little uncomfortable. 'I was about to come over and say hello but I didn't want to disturb you.'

'Well, I'm very glad to see you. I've been meaning

to come and see you.' He swats at a wasp that is buzzing around the flap of his hat. 'I want to apologise for the fire.'

'No need. Not your fault. I gather it was a spark from a tractor.'

'Yes, but we all know these things can happen in the dry and my man should have had precautions in place. I'm so sorry about the church.'

'I put it on the market.' He must surely have heard.

'Fire damage?'

'No. It cleaned up relatively well. Except for the windows, but that will be for the new buyer to deal with.'

'I'm sorry to hear that. They're very fine windows, much admired over the years. My great-great-grandfather installed them and he was very particular about such things.'

The young woman is looking down from her rock and McAlister beckons her over. 'My daughter, Lily,' he says. 'This is Mrs North, who bought St Martin's.' And then to Zoe: 'I'm teaching her to fish. Couldn't get her interested to start with but she's come around.'

Zoe recognises her now as the girl in the car on the night that she and Neville had encountered McAlister at the church gates. She has a narrow face, with strong bones and a sallow tan. In her pale blue eyes there is a disconcerting glare of suspicion, of unfocussed hostility. 'I need more practice,' she says, politely.

'That's all it is,' says McAlister, 'practice and more

practice. And learning to read the river.'

In his tone he is a little too hearty. His manner, so resolutely matter-of-fact, cannot conceal the intensity of his concern for his daughter. Zoe is moved, despite herself, by his barely disguised fear of helplessness. He is desperate to cure Lily of her sadness, using whatever means he has at his disposal, perhaps the only means left to him given that nothing else has so far worked.

She is prompted to put him at his ease. 'Do you eat the trout?'

'Occasionally. Not mad on them, and neither is Lily. Sometimes we keep one. Pass it on as a gift.' He pauses. 'May I ask, Mrs North, if you're planning to leave us?'

'No, I like it here. I'm looking for a small piece of land to build on. On a rise if I can get it.'

'Very wise. But not easy to come by, with all these tree-changers moving in. I'll keep an eye out for you.'

'Thank you, that's very kind.'

He turns to his daughter. 'Well, Lily, back to it, eh?'

With no desire to linger, Zoe begins her walk back to the chalet, along the rough track that leads to the road. In her head she carries the soothing stream of the river, a soundtrack to her wandering thoughts, and what she is reminded of now is the coalminer Ron, with whom she had spoken at Gail McVilly's dinner: the man with the blue marlin. 'We throw them back,' he said. And now the man with the trout, lowering it gently into the river.

What is this strange relationship with the fish? Why hunt if there is to be no kill? Why torment the fish? The hours of practice, the infinite patience—for what? Never mind, for it's possible the daughter will master the delicate art of casting, and in the act of unfurling the perfect line will release her sadness into the fish's mouth.

36

Zoe has worked late. There is now on Thursday nights an evening clinic. She has parked in the main street of the town to buy her supper at the kebab shop and there, on the kerb outside the shop, waiting to cross the road, is Melanie Doyle.

Melanie has her back to Zoe and either has not seen her or is pretending not to, and Zoe walks to the edge of the kerb and taps the young woman on the shoulder. 'I hear you've resigned and moved out to Beralga,' she says.

'Oh, hi. How are you, Zoe?'

'More to the point, how are you?'

'I burnt out. I needed a change.'

Some change, she thinks, but will not pry. Now is not the time. 'Come and see me. When you have the time. I'm at Gail McVilly's place for the time being. The church was damaged in a fire.'

'I heard. Shame.'

'I sold it. A young couple from the city are turning it into a restaurant.'

'Really?' Melanie shakes her head. 'Tell them to buy our pork. Best bacon there is.'

Now she is moved to grasp Melanie's arm, to grasp it hard and to say, furiously: *Don't be flippant with me, Melanie, it doesn't become you.* But restrains herself, because what she really wants to say is: *Thank you, Melanie,* and *You'll never know.* Instead, she smiles, the patronising smile of the older woman. 'So you've given up being a sort-of vegetarian, Melanie.'

'Never was, Zoe, never was.'

'I would like you to have come and told me of your plans.'

'I meant to.'

No, you didn't. Why is she being evasive? It's so unlike her. Zoe might construe this as dishonest; at the very least it is out of character. Before, in her role as theatre director, Melanie had spilled into every corner, had asserted her will with an energetic charge that seemed able to conjure whatever she needed from thin air, or at least out of her collection of discarded objects that she could meld into new forms. But now Melanie is responding to her with a deadpan reserve, like an actor who has lost interest in her audience. And doesn't this go against the grain? Are not the newly converted keen to proselytise, to tell their story, their eyes alight with revelation, their faces lit with a rapturous glow? But Melanie is withholding.

'I hope you will come and see me one day.'

'Sure.' The word hovers there, like a verbal shrug.

Zoe opens her mouth to say more but the lights change.

With a distant gaze and her hand raised in a half-salute, Melanie steps off the kerb.

37

So here she is now, back where she began, like the ouro-boros, the mythological snake that swallows its own tail.

Lachie has sent her links to kit homes and she is sitting up late and trawling the net for possibilities. Possibility: the word lodges in her inner ear like a small crystal egg, cool and sharp-edged.

There has been an explosion in the design of pre-fabricated and small dwellings and a proliferation of websites to market them, many with jocular titles: *Choose Simplicity over Size*, *Size Doesn't Count* and *Living Big in a Tiny House*. What would it mean, she wonders, to live big? To build anything will use up her remaining capital, but at least she will not have to deal with the problem of renovation, of what to do with redundant space.

Meanwhile, she is intrigued by the evangelical pitch of the websites, how they proselytise for a new form of virtuous living, a holy minimalism that declares itself 'in harmony with the natural world'. We have sinned, they say, though only by implication since the accent always is on the positive; we have lost control of nature, or rather the delusion that we ever had it, and now we must live the simple life. They assume that she, the buyer, is either a convert or jaded; they invite her to 'recharge your spirit in the natural world, to join the ranks of the enchanted'. Though the houses are small, they are semi-transparent: walls of glass and clerestory panels along the roof line. 'Light pours through the panoramic windows that blur the line between indoor and outdoor…Now you can feel that you are living in another reality with little dividing you from the world of air, light and forest.' As much as possible, inside and outside can be made to meld. The old idea of home as a defensive enclosure is for the fearful and the unenlightened. There is even a small house on display with a bedroom entirely of glass, like a greenhouse in which, presumably, the human body in repose can bloom overnight. 'Small but spatially rich.' As for the interiors, these are expanses of grey and white (the 'magic of monochrome'). Without exception they feature, 'crisp clean lines' or boast of 'perpendicular trajectories of light and air' that create 'a platform for possibility'. And all with not an icon in sight.

Except that the house is the icon. Here is an inverted pitched roof 'inspired by seagull wings'. Another roof is compared to the wings of a butterfly; another is said to recall a folded leaf. The tone is serious but playful: a lime-green Swedish home 'looks just like a Monopoly house'. The architect of another has been inspired by nomadic yurt dwellers. There are many iterations of the log cabin, as if they are all pioneers in a new world, out to lead the simple life, only now with sustainable timbers, passive solar, rooftop panels, water-efficient systems and modules that come in flat packs and can be assembled like Lego. (One ingeniously designed cabin, off grid in the desert, is touted as 'apocalypse proof', but this is a jarring note, rarely struck.)

And yet the copywriters for these sites have a preacher's gift: their phrases land on the ear like magical incantations, a litany devoted to the sacrament of dwelling and the new religion of nature, a religion without the burden of a troublesome history, for the ideal small house makes no territorial claim; it is unassuming, and it is infinitely mobile: 'you just park it somewhere pretty and let the interiors fade away'.

Ah, but here is something more ambitious, a small house with a vaulting ceiling not unlike that of a church: a 'perfect sanctuary'. And lest this sound unnervingly unworldly, it is said, nevertheless, to feature a 'robust materiality', which, Zoe supposes, it would have since presumably it's not built of floss. But it's true that some offerings are flimsier than others, like the tiny biodegradable cabin suspended on a foundation of eleven poles with a wooden skeleton that can be assembled in seven days, so odd an object that one night it invades her dreams, stalking the bush and moving silently through the scrub like an alien being looking for a place to settle without trespass.

On a visit to Mick and Berenice she describes her search.

'Good idea,' says Berenice, 'like a cubby house for grown-ups, eh?'

But Mick is dismissive. 'They're rubbish—they don't last. If you want to go alternative, use concrete and stone. One of them hippie numbers.'

'But that would be expensive.'

'Depends,' he says. 'Know a builder who'd give you a good quote.'

That night, unable to sleep, she pulls a coat over her night-dress and, taking a torch, steps out onto the dry turf. Below her, on its grassy terrace, sits the old cast-iron bath planted with marigolds and the white enamelled sheen of its rim gives off a faint glow. The air is cool, a light breeze ruffles her hair and she walks down to sit on the wooden bench beside the bath. Here she can feel the boundaries of the world around her dissolve, all thought abandoned and her senses heightened so that she might hear only the light pad of a wallaby, the snarl of a possum or the hoarse breathing of a creature unknown to her. But not tonight. Tonight her thoughts are of Melanie Doyle and her conversion. She would not say she has been troubled by it, merely baffled. Had Melanie in some way been affected by the perfor-mances in the church or, rather, not the performances but the church itself? Had it suggested a void of meaning in her life? Or was she reacting to criticism from parents for mounting an unsuitable play? Surely not. Melanie was the last person to be affected by her critics. She had set out to defy them and anticipated their disapproval. No, like Nick, she was looking for something more, something beyond what passes for normal life, some intensity of focus, a unity of resolve she could share with others.

There are moments, to her surprise, when she misses the church: its lingering smell of incense and wood; the artisanal charm of its masonry that sometimes drew her to press her palms against the warm, stippled surface of the stone. At odd times an image of the play will flare in her mind's eye: the girls in their Grecian folds; Travis Hanlon declaiming from the steps of the sanctuary; Melanie perched on her stool, earnestly making notes; and all of them lit by the warm evening light in the nave.

Above her now, the night sky is clear, the stars diamond-cut. A chill has settled on the air and, drawing her coat around her, she leans into the high back of the garden seat and looks out at the shadowy outline of the hills, feeling almost that she is sitting on the rim of the earth. And how did she arrive here in this fugitive nest above a blur of olive trees? What remains of the young Zoe North? Only, it seems, her perverse fate, a fine thread in the tangled skein of an unquiet world.

The night before, Lachie had rung to ask if she had made any plans, and she had told him that all she can decide on for now is a gabled roof and a deck.

'You haven't got far, then?'

'How could I? First, I need to find the land. You know, orientation and all that.'

'No clues?'

'Well, one. I'm going to have a stained-glass window.'

Lachie had laughed. 'Got a taste for them now, have you?'

'Not exactly.' She had told him about the local glass-maker, Stefan Hennessey—he who is reconfiguring the windows of St Martin's—and how she was thinking she would commission him to make a window of a single black cockatoo. But in speaking to Lachie she realised it would have to be a pair, since they are never seen alone, though the work involved in making a pair will mean more expense.

Still, they have always been her favourite bird, hers and Nick's, and no matter the design of the small house she will one day build, she will have her icon. The valley is still in drought and the flight of the black cockatoo is said to be a harbinger of rain.